Chosen by the Sheikh.
He *always* gets what he wants.

Passion blazes fiercer than the burning sun when
two ruthless sheikhs claim new royal bedmates!

Chosen for pleasure, can these women tame the
wild hearts of their desert lords?

Feel the heat in these two scorching stories
from *USA TODAY* bestselling authors,

Kim Lawrence

and

Lynn Raye Harris

All about the authors...

KIM LAWRENCE lives on a farm in rural Anglesey. She runs two miles daily and finds this an excellent opportunity to unwind and seek inspiration for her writing! It also helps her keep up with her husband, two active sons and the various stray animals that have adopted them. Always a fanatical consumer of fiction, she is now equally enthusiastic about writing. She loves a happy ending!

LYNN RAYE HARRIS read her first Harlequin® romance when her grandmother carted home a box from a yard sale. She didn't know she wanted to be a writer then, but she definitely knew she wanted to marry a sheikh or a prince, and live the glamorous life she read about in the pages. Instead, she married a military man and moved around the world. These days she makes her home in north Alabama, with her handsome husband and two crazy cats. Writing for Harlequin is a dream come true. You can visit her at www.lynnrayeharris.com.

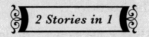

2 Stories in 1

Kim Lawrence
Lynn Raye Harris
CHOSEN BY THE SHEIKH

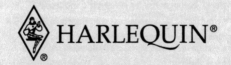

HARLEQUIN®

TORONTO • NEW YORK • LONDON
AMSTERDAM • PARIS • SYDNEY • HAMBURG
STOCKHOLM • ATHENS • TOKYO • MILAN • MADRID
PRAGUE • WARSAW • BUDAPEST • AUCKLAND

Recycling programs
for this product may
not exist in your area.

ISBN-13: 978-0-373-12954-6

CHOSEN BY THE SHEIKH
Copyright © 2010 by Harlequin Enterprises Ltd.

First North American Publication 2010.

The publisher acknowledges the copyright holders of the individual
works as follows:

THE SHEIKH AND THE VIRGIN
Copyright © 2008 by Kim Lawrence.

KEPT FOR THE SHEIKH'S PLEASURE
Copyright © 2010 by Lynn Raye Harris.

CONTENTS

THE SHEIKH AND
THE VIRGIN

Kim Lawrence

CHAPTER ONE

'SHOW her directly in when she arrives,' Tariq said, handing the lawyer a photograph. 'This is her.'

James Sinclair glanced at the badly focused holiday snapshot of three people. At the centre of the laughing group on the beach was a young dark-haired man, who had his arms around two young women, one either side of him.

James tilted his head to look up at the tall dark-haired figure in the impeccably tailored suit before him. His secretary's words came back to him. She had assured him, in an uncharacteristically giggly moment, that the women in the building weren't interested in the suit the Prince wore, more in the body it covered.

'Which woman are you expecting, Prince Tariq?' The lawyer's manner was respectful and, though he tried to hide it, nervous, as his glance slid from one pretty bikini-clad figure to the other.

Relax, James, he told himself. He genuinely thought he might feel similarly edgy if someone had left him in a room with an unchained and hungry panther. In fact now that he thought of it there was something about this man that brought that sleek, dangerous and unpredictable animal to mind.

If the business they did on behalf of the Royal family of Zarhat hadn't been worth several small fortunes to the law firm he worked for, he might have been tempted to delegate this task. The heir apparent to Zarhat's throne made him feel about as confident as a fresh-faced intern—not a pleasant feeling for a man who was acknowledged as one of the best litigators of his generation.

When he spoke Prince Tariq Al Kamal's English was impeccable, distinguished only by the slightest of accents. But right now the incredulity in his deep voice was more noticeable than the foreign inflection. 'Which woman?'

James lifted his eyes, connecting with those of the younger man standing before him, who was a good six inches taller than him. It was a struggle to keep his gaze level.

Continuing to feel uncharacteristically uneasy and unsure, James wondered if it was a power thing. But he suspected that even if he'd had no knowledge of the Al Kamal wealth and influence he would have instinctively known that here was a man he didn't want to be on the wrong side of…

James considered the other man's lean dark face and thought…*implacable*.

This guy, he mused, would not be gentle when it came to removing something or someone who got in his way.

Probably four or five years younger than his own thirty-seven years, James decided, studying his sable-haired client surreptitiously, the guy really looked the part. He was handsome as hell, clearly with an intellect to match his golden-skinned good-looks. James laid a hand to his own slightly generous middle and thought, I really should make some time for squash…

Tariq raised one dark brow as he studied the lawyer. The man's credentials were impeccable, but after a question like that it was hard not to wonder if he was all he was cracked up to be.

Which woman?

Which woman did he think? He took the photo back and glanced down, his dark, veiled gaze sliding over the blonde and his brother before coming to rest on the redhead. The blonde was pretty, in a cutesy, curvy, giggly sort of way. No. He dismissed her with a mental click of his long brown fingers. She was hardly the type of female who would make a man such as his brother forget the responsibilities that had been drilled into him since his childhood. The responsibilities they had both been taught came hand in hand with privilege.

Now, the second female—with the tousled titian curls, seductive mouth and alabaster skin—*she* was such a woman.

Yes, she was definitely a woman who could inspire a little madness in a man. As for responsibilities… This woman could probably, without much exertion, make a man forget his name!

As his eyes lingered on the redhead's vivid laughing face he felt his irritation fade. It really wasn't hard, he conceded reluctantly, to see why his little brother Khalid had lost his head and his heart to this woman. Even in a blurry snapshot her earthy sex appeal hit you straight between the eyes—not to mention other places further south!

She did not have a conventionally beautiful face. Her rounded chin was too firm, the skin across the bridge of her small, slightly tip-tilted nose was lightly freckled, and her smiling sensuously curved lips were too wide. But the exotic slant of her big long-lashed eyes gave her features an almost feline look and certainly a sensual quality.

His glance dropped to her body. She was tall, square-shouldered and full-bosomed. She had an hourglass figure, and the flare of her full hips was perfectly balanced by her long shapely legs. The skin his brother's fingers touched in the photograph was milky pale.

Her skin would be warm and smooth under a man's touch, infinitely delectable…Tariq put aside the distracting image, his expression instantly hardening. That man was not going to be Khalid.

His little brother was clearly not thinking with his brain. If Khalid had gone out looking for the most unsuitable bride alive he could not have found one who fitted the bill better than this redhead.

She had no family; there was not even a father's name on her birth certificate. And, while he did not hold her background against him, it was to him highly significant that after the death of her mother, she had never settled with any of the numerous foster families she had been placed in. This was a pattern that had continued into adulthood, and she had travelled the world working. Tariq could not fault her work ethic, but she had never accumulated any money or possessions, and she had never stayed in one place long enough to put down roots.

It was totally inconceivable that such a woman could fill the role of Royal Princess.

Tariq returned his attention back to the lawyer. 'The red-head,' he said, dispensing the blatantly unnecessary information with impatience as he slid the photo back into his breast pocket.

Dragging his long brown fingers over his bare dark head, he slid his dark pewter-flecked gaze to the window. It was closed and he was conscious of the feeling of claustrophobia he often felt when in London, or in any other major city for that matter.

At home his office windows would be flung wide open, allowing the warm desert breeze to circulate. Set in the oldest part of the palace complex, his office was located in the highest tower, and it offered panoramic views out over the old town, stretching as far as the new town, with its shiny glass-fronted buildings, then out further to the desert and mountains beyond.

Almost imperceptibly he felt some of the tension in his shoulders lessen. Tension that had been gradually building since he had providentially discovered his brother was about to make a disastrous marriage.

Tonight he would return home and be standing in that room, watching the sunset.

He had been looking at spectacular sunsets over the desert all his life, but familiarity had not bred contempt. The flame sky never failed to move something deep inside him, reminding him of the connection he felt to the land and its people, both of which his family had held in trust for many generations.

Some men might have termed the connection spiritual, but

Tariq felt no need to put a name to it. It was just an integral part of him.

'Just show her through when she arrives,' Tariq informed the departing lawyer. Time was of the essence, and the sooner he nipped this sentimental and unsuitable romance in the bud the better.

Pressing a long finger to the indentation above his aquiline nose, Tariq felt that tension between his shoulderblades creep back. Damn Khalid! The planes of his strongly sculpted face tautened as he dwelt on the secret plans of his normally cautious and co-operative brother.

When their own English mother had chosen her freedom over her children, Khalid, who had been three at the time, had crept into his big brother's bed each night for months after to cry himself to sleep. How, Tariq wondered, could a child of such a disastrous union, who had suffered so much as a child, not now realise that it was impossible to combine two cultures?

Maybe, Tariq brooded, it was some genetic defect? Their father was a man whose actions had always been characterised by strength and rational thought; he had shown inexplicable weakness and lack of judgement in only one thing—love.

Well, if this was a genetic flaw, and the weakness surfaced in him, Tariq, he had no doubt that he would be able to subdue it. Tariq was a man who prided himself on his iron control. It would not even occur to him to follow such selfish impulses. He had no immediate marriage plans, but when he did eventually commit himself Tariq knew his choice of consort would not be a woman who had split loyalties. Not for him a woman who could not or would not adapt to her new life in a foreign land.

No, he would marry a woman—when the time came—who would stand beside him as he continued the onerous task of bringing modern reforms to their ancient kingdom and its rich diverse cultural heritage. Love, too often in his opinion, was used as an excuse for inappropriate behaviour, and would be very low down the list when he came to look for a suitable bride for himself.

* * *

The lawyer guided her through a series of interconnected rooms, and when they reached the last he stood back and indicated to Beatrice that she should go inside.

In the doorway she turned to call out to the retreating figure. 'Look, what is this all about…?'

A stranger's rough velvet voice from inside the room cut across her bemused protest.

'Just come in, Miss Devlin.'

Cautiously Beatrice responded to the terse instruction and stepped into the room. Her inspection of her surroundings only got as far as the figure seated behind the desk. He rose as she stepped forward: a seriously tall man, lean, long of leg and broad of shoulder.

He was also young and sinfully good-looking, if you liked the dark fallen angel look, and frankly, Beatrice thought staring, who wouldn't?

'Take a seat.' He commanded, in that velvet voice again.

'I'm sorry—I don't know who you are, or—'

'I doubt that…' His long lashes brushed against the sharp angles of his chiselled cheekbones as his midnight glance dipped, skimming the lush contours of her body.

By the time his attention returned to her face Beatrice knew her cheeks were burning in reaction. There was something of a calculated insult in his insolent scrutiny.

Later she might be bewildered by his attitude, but right now Beatrice was too furious for analysis. Was he trying to make her lose her temper? Or was he always this obnoxiously rude? Well, either way she wouldn't give him the satisfaction of responding.

Beatrice lifted her chin, raised her brows in a quizzical fashion and gave him a calm smile. 'Manners really aren't your strong point, are they…?' She murmured amusedly before pulling out a chair. 'I'm assuming I wasn't summoned here just so that you could insult me…?'

She was rewarded by a perplexed frown that twitched his strongly defined sable brows into a straight line above his hawkish nose. The frown stayed in place as he watched her settle herself in the chair and casually cross one slender ankle over the other. It was a scrutiny that Beatrice was painfully conscious of. She was equally determined not to betray the fact.

This was not a person to show weakness to. The man was clearly a barbarian, she decided, and no amount of tailoring could disguise the fact. As mad as she was with him, for looking at her as though she were a piece of meat, she was madder with herself for responding on some primal level to the raw sexual challenge in his stance.

Cut yourself some slack, she counselled herself, as she slowed her breathing to a less agitated level. The man does have more undiluted blatant sexuality in his little finger than the average male has in his entire body. Her eyes skimmed the long lean length of him again, and she stifled an internal sigh. Whatever else the man was, there was nothing about him physically that she could find fault with.

Finally he stopped his appraisal of her and spoke. 'You look like a smart girl.' You only had to look into those green eyes to see this woman was no fool. Though admittedly intelligence was not the first thing that hit a man when this woman walked into a room.

Since the moment she had strolled in, with a sway of those feminine hips, filling the small room with the scent of roses and rain, he had been more than conscious of the sexual allure she radiated.

Beatrice flashed her white teeth in an insincere smile. 'Thank you,' she murmured, but she was not making the mistake of assuming this was a compliment.

It was pretty hard to think that when he was looking at her as though she was something unpleasant he'd discovered on his shoe! She wondered idly what he'd look like when he wasn't sneering.

It seemed doubtful, given the inexplicable antagonism vibrating in the air between them, that she was ever going to find out. But, despite this, her wilful imagination toyed with a mental image of those arrogant patrician features relaxed in a genuine smile. The corners of his wide sensual lips pulled upwards, maybe a few sexy crinkles at the corners of those sensational eyes, and the temperature on those silver-flecked depths a few degrees above zero...

'And as a smart girl I'm sure you already know why I arranged this meeting.' He slowly folded his long lean length gracefully into the chair behind the desk. 'Let's lay our cards on the table.'

No cards, but his hands lay on the mahogany surface of the desk that stood between them. His tapering fingers were long and brown, and exerted a fascination for Beatrice that she was beginning to think bordered on the unhealthy.

'My brother plans to marry you.'

Beatrice's head came up with a jerk that jarred her spine. Eyes as hard as obsidian that were lightened only by those strange silvery flecks bored into her.

If she had any remaining doubts that this was a case of mistaken identity, this bizarre statement washed them away.

'I'm not marrying anyone's brother,' she promised him.

Irritation chased across his lean features. 'Then this is not you?' he drawled.

Beatrice looked suspiciously for a moment at the item he extracted from a file and placed on her side of the desk before she picked it up.

Her eyebrows almost hit her hairline when she recognised the holiday snap. It had been taken two summers earlier, when she had been working as an au pair in the South of France.

The two people with her on the beach were friends she had met that summer. Emma, whose father had owned the villa next to hers, and Khalid, the charming young man Emma had introduced her to.

Both had remained her friends—in fact her sleeping bag was at present on the sofa in Emma's London flat.

Her narrowed eyes left the photo and flew to the man's face. 'How did you get this?'

He dismissed the question with a shrug of his powerful shoulders. 'That is not relevant.'

Strange men with photos of her in a bikini were extremely relevant to Beatrice!

'I do not normally concern myself with my brother's holiday romances.'

'Your brother... Khalid is your brother? Then that makes you...' She swallowed, her voice trailing off. That made him Tariq Al Kamal, heir to the throne of one of the richest countries in the world.

This incredible information certainly explained the autocratic air and the imperious arrogance she had been witness to since she had arrived.

Not that Beatrice was impressed. Why be impressed by an accident of birth? This man had been handed everything on a plate. Beatrice, on the other hand, had worked for everything she had. The way she saw it, the people who had been born to wealth and privilege should be required to prove themselves, not the other way around.

Khalid was the most self-deprecating *un*-royal person you could ever imagine meeting. The summer she had spent with Emma and him had been half over before Emma had discovered by accident his royal connection. A connection that he had typically played down.

'Sorry, if I'd known who you were I'd have curtsied.' Which no doubt he'd take as his due. God, the man was everything she detested most wrapped up in one package!

A gorgeous package, admittedly. Her glance drifted as he shrugged off his jacket. The suggestive dark shadowy triangle on his chest, visible beneath the fine white fabric of his shirt, sent an embarrassing rush of heat through her.

'Forget the pretence, Miss Devlin.'

Forget the body, Beatrice.

'I am aware of your relationship with my brother.'

She didn't have the faintest idea how the man had got the idea she and Khalid were an item—Emma would laugh when she shared the joke—but it was definitely time she put an end to this farce and got out of here.

'Look, I know Khalid—sure.' She spread her hands

in a pacifying gesture and raised her eyes to his. 'He's a friend, but—'

'Men and women are not *friends*.'

Beatrice couldn't restrain herself. He clearly thought his opinion on any given subject was definitive. 'And you'd know all about friendship…?'

His sensuous mouth curled. 'I know all about women,' he corrected.

Now, that, she admitted, was easy to believe. Combating a fresh rush of cheek-burning colour, she tore her gaze from the sensual outline of his lips and pleaded sarcastically, 'Spare me the tales of your conquests.' The last thing she needed was any more fuel for the images already playing in her head!

His lips thinned in distaste and he qualified, 'I know all about women like you. I know of your ambitions.'

His voice dropped to a menacing purr that did painful things to her sensitive nerve-endings as he leaned forward and added softly, 'Let me tell you it is not going to happen, Miss Devlin. You will not trap my brother into marriage.'

'Is that a threat?' Daft question. Of course it was a threat. And Beatrice responded the same way she always did when she came across someone who thought they could intimidate her. She saw red and came out fighting.

'Trap, you said…?' She pressed a finger to the suggestion of a cleft in her softly rounded chin and pretended to consider the comment. 'Get pregnant, you mean…? I actually hadn't thought of that,' she admitted, before throwing back her head and loosing a husky laugh of amusement.

His dark face tautened with anger, the golden skin pulling tight across his prominent cheekbones as his contemptuous eyes locked onto her face. 'You would be wise not to consider such a thing.'

'And you would be wise to keep your opinions and your orders and your damned condescending attitude to yourself!' she retorted, rising to her feet and fixing him with a wrathful glare.

'How dare you speak to me in that way?'

An overload of adrenaline was still pumping through her veins, and his astonished demand made no impact on her.

'Don't you think your brother is old enough to decide who he marries?' She for one pitied the woman—who would presumably need to gain this man's approval. 'I don't see there's much you can do about it.' Except strangle me. And he looked quite capable of doing that!

'I am not an unreasonable man.'

But he was definitely a very angry one, she thought, her eyes glued to the erratic pulse that clenched and unclenched in his lean cheek.

'I can see that you should be compensated for the time and energy you have put into this…project.'

'Project?'

'I think you'll find I am quite generous,' he replied smoothly as he pushed a piece of paper across the table towards her. 'Feel free to consult a lawyer, but it is quite straightforward. Once you sign this agreement, stating you will not marry my brother and you will not make any further attempt to contact him, you will receive half that stated amount. Six months later you will receive the balance.'

'You're bribing me?' And just when she'd thought this situation couldn't get any more surreal!

'I am offering you financial compensation.'

'You want to pay me off?'

'I am willing to pay to remove you from my brother's life,' he admitted, clearly irritated by her insistence on calling a spade a spade.

'I'd starve before I'd take a penny off you!' she flared, fixing him with a furious smoky glare.

He looked taken aback by her anger. 'There is, I think you will find, rather more than a penny on the table.'

Her lips curled contemptuously as she glanced down. 'This isn't about the amount.' He clearly didn't have the faintest idea he had just offered her an insult. 'I don't care how— Good God!' she gasped, catching sight of the figure.

Her round eyes moved from the paper to the man behind the

desk, who was watching her with an air of smug complacence. It had obviously never even crossed his mind that she would say no.

'That's a lot of money,' she admitted, with massive under-statement. 'But actually I've not a lot of use for it. However, being a princess...well, that's something that money can't buy, isn't it...?'

His eyes narrowed to icy slits as he rose majestically to his feet.

She had to tilt her head back to look at him, and her taunting smile dimmed.

'That, Miss Devlin, will not happen,' he told her positively.

'We'll see...'

'If you are trying to extract more money...?' he began grimly.

'I'm not. The fact is,' she said stabbing her finger in the direction of his chest, 'you don't have enough money to buy me. I'm sure you've spent your life throwing money at problems to make them go away, but me—I'm not for sale. At any price.'

Her regal exit was slightly marred by the fact that her hands were shaking so much it took her three attempts to open the door.

The irony was, of course, that his insults and his bribe were not really intended for her. He had made a huge mistake. She just hoped that when he discovered Khalid's real girlfriend the other girl would have the guts to tell him to go to hell too.

CHAPTER TWO

'ARE you all right, miss?'

It required a supreme effort, but Bea forced a smile as she turned to the concerned-looking silver-haired man who had stopped to make the anxious enquiry. Concerned people who gave a damn were rare commodities nowadays, and in her opinion deserved at least a smile.

'I'm fine, thank you,' she promised.

He didn't look entirely convinced, and if she looked anything like she felt, Beatrice wasn't surprised.

'Perhaps you should sit down…? A glass of water…?' He glanced towards the large impressive-looking building Beatrice had just emerged from.

'Really, I'm fine,' she insisted, able to hide her shaking hands in the pockets of her jacket, but unable to control the emotional quiver in her voice.

In truth, she had never felt less fine. She was, in fact, furious. A laid-back, easygoing person, Beatrice rarely lost her temper—but when she did she lost it big time!

She remained so angry that her furious long-legged stride got her back to Emma's flat in record time. Turning the key in the lock, she pushed open the door and stepped into the sitting room.

'You'll never guess what—' She stopped abruptly. The room was empty, but a muffled sound from the bedroom indicated her friend was home.

'That didn't take long,' Emma said, belting a robe around

her waist as she emerged from the bedroom, her blonde curls tousled and her cheeks flushed. 'Well, what was your meeting all about? Has a rich relative left you a fortune?'

Bea, struggling to control her anger, barely registered her friend's breathless voice as she gritted her teeth. 'A fortune was involved,' she admitted, kicking off her shoes and flopping down onto the sofa. 'But, like I told you, I don't have any relatives—rich or otherwise.'

Neither, after living in foster care after her mother's death, did she have Emma's romantic imagination.

Bea had responded to the mysterious invitation that had arrived in the post with curiosity and an open mind, but no great expectations. Definitely not the expectation of being insulted so comprehensively!

'Neither did I bump into a white knight at the corner shop.'

'Don't be like that, Bea. There's someone out there for you...a soul mate.'

Sometimes Emma's incurable romanticism could be irritating. 'I won't hold my breath—' She stopped, tilting her head in a listening attitude. 'Did you hear that? It sounded as if it came—'

Emma threw a nervous look at the closed bedroom door, before perching on the arm of a chair and asking quickly, 'What on earth did the lawyer say to put you in this mood?'

'It wasn't the lawyer I spoke to. The man I did speak to offered me a small fortune.'

Actually, Beatrice thought, not so small! The number of noughts on the paper he had handed her had looked like a misprint, but apparently it wasn't.

Emma looked bemused. 'And that made you angry?'

'The money was conditional on me... I warn you, Emma, you're not going to believe this.' She unclenched her fists, sucked in a deep breath and tried to smile—it really was absurd. 'It was conditional on me not marrying Khalid!'

She paused, fully expecting Emma's incredulous laughter, but not expecting to see the colour seep from her friend's face.

'What did he say when you told him you weren't engaged to Khalid?'

'He didn't give me the chance. And then I got so mad, because he was so utterly detestable and smug, and… Well,' she admitted ruefully, 'I lost my temper and told him I fancied the idea of being a princess. Princess Bea…' She struck a pose and chuckled. 'What do you think? Shall I suggest it to Khalid? Incidentally, I must give him a ring and warn him what his brother is up to.'

'Oh, God, Bea!' Emma moaned, looking if it was at all possible, even paler. 'Why did you say that to him…?'

Beatrice was perplexed by her friend's attitude. 'Could it have had something to do with the fact the man treated me like some cheap little tart? I don't think you understand, Emma.' Beatrice spelt it out. 'Poor Khalid must have fallen in love with some girl. His brother is trying to buy this girl off, and for some weird reason he thinks it's me.' She laughed, lifting her hair from the back of her neck and stretching with feline grace. 'Weird doesn't really cover it.'

'Oh, Emma understands, Bea.'

At the sound of the rueful voice Beatrice jumped up—in time to see Khalid emerge from the bedroom, his shirt unbuttoned to reveal his bronzed torso.

'Khalid…?' She looked blankly from the man in the doorway to her friend and back again. 'But you're…' Colour flooded her face as comprehension dawned. 'How long?' She stopped and shook her head. 'Never mind. It's none of my business.'

Emma looked stricken. 'We wanted to tell you, Bea, but…'

Khalid put a protective hand on Emma's shoulder. 'Tariq and my family have very traditional views on this matter.'

Things were slowly beginning to sink in for Beatrice. 'I knew something was going on, but I never—' She stopped, her eyes widening. 'So you and Emma—you're getting married?'

Beatrice watched her friend struggle with tears as she glanced at her lover. 'It's difficult,' she said unhappily.

'Yes, we are getting married,' Khalid contradicted her,

sounding firm. He sounded less firm as he added bleakly, 'Somehow.'

How difficult could it be?

Beatrice bit her tongue and forced a smile. 'That's…' She was still finding it hard to get her head around the situation, but now she thought about it, it made perfect sense. Khalid and Emma made a perfect couple. 'It really is fantastic news.'

Well, it would be if you took one apparently oppressive and old-fashioned sibling out of the picture.

Frowning, she expressed her bewilderment and indignation out loud. 'What is your brother's problem anyway? He's the one who's going to be King, isn't he? Why does it matter who you marry?'

'Tariq is King in all but name. Since our father had his stroke he isn't seen in public.'

'If it *was* me you were going to marry I could understand.' Beatrice could see realistically that she wasn't anyone's idea of a royal bride. 'But Emma. Well…if I said you could do better, Khalid, I'd be lying. Emma is perfect.'

'I think so,' Khalid agreed.

The glow in his eyes as he looked at his prospective bride brought a lump to Beatrice's throat. She had to do something for them. They were meant to be together.

'Tariq has strong views about marriage. He thinks we shouldn't marry—'

'Beneath you?' Beatrice cut in, unable to repress the bitter retort. 'Yes, I sort of got that.'

'It's not that… Our mother was English, and when our parents' marriage broke up it was pretty rough. I was small, so I don't really remember, but I think that it made a big impact on Tariq. When they finally split up she came back to England. She wasn't allowed to take us with her.'

'That must have been terrible for her.' And pretty tough on the boys, deprived of their mother, she privately conceded.

'We saw her in the holidays or I did. Tariq always refused to see her and our half sister—then there was the accident.'

'He blamed her,' Emma, who clearly knew the story, explained.

'You said the accident…?'

'A car smash on the motorway. She was killed instantly.'

'I'm sorry, Khalid,' Beatrice said, her tender heart touched by the story.

Not that it offered any excuses for the dreadful brother's behaviour. She too had lost her own mother, at a similar age, but it didn't make her feel she could go around sitting in judgement on total strangers!

Khalid took Emma's hand. 'And I'm sorry, Bea—that you had to go through that with Tariq.'

'Better me than Em,' Beatrice retorted, adding with a shrug, 'I was mad, not hurt.'

'Tariq will love Emma once he meets her. It just has to be the right time.'

Beatrice's heart went out to the unhappy lovers. From her experience that morning, she was pretty certain that the right time would be of the 'when hell freezes over' variety, and from Khalid's expression she was sure that he knew it too.

She felt a surge of frustration. She'd been hoping that she could laugh off this morning, but that was before she knew what was at stake.

'There must be something I can do or say to this brother of yours.' A brother who seemed to live in another century and who thought everyone had a price. Then it hit her. The solution was right under their noses and so blindingly simple that they couldn't see it!

'He'll never accept me,' Emma retorted bleakly. 'Khalid would have to choose between me and his family, and I couldn't let him do that.'

'What if there was another way?'

The lovers looked at her with a mixture of doubt and hope.

'He might see you, Em, in a entirely new light if he's just endured a visit from the bride from hell.' Bea's green eyes, dancing with devilish excitement, were at stark variance with her butter-wouldn't-melt expression. She smiled at the bemused-looking couple. 'It's perfect,' she enthused as she warmed to the idea forming in her head.

'What are you talking about, Bea?' Khalid asked impatiently.

'Don't ask,' Emma advised. 'Look at her face—she's got one of her crazy plans.'

'Not crazy—perfect!' Beatrice insisted, punching the air in a triumphant gesture. 'It can't fail. And the beauty is that it was his idea, so we're just going along with it. Take me home with you, Khalid.'

'What?'

'I'll be the fiancée your brother thinks I am, and when you dump me they'll be so relieved that anyone else you bring home will seem perfect,' she promised grimly.

And the other beauty of her plan was that she would be able to exact revenge first-hand on the wretched man.

'She's serious?' Khalid said, looking to Emma for confirmation.

'Totally,' Beatrice promised them both. She arched a feathery brow and looked at Khalid. 'Unless you have a better idea?'

'It's hard. Family is...'

Hearing the defensive note in her young friend's voice, Beatrice smiled and admitted readily, 'Something I know zilch about.' At times like this that didn't seem such a bad thing, even though when she was growing up a family and roots had been the only things she'd dreamt of.

'If we do this crazy thing and it backfires...Tariq realises what we're up to...it will only make things worse,' Khalid said, shaking his head.

'How?' Emma said in a small voice.

Khalid looked at her.

'How can it be worse than this?' she asked in a stricken whisper. 'Tell me, Khalid, what is worse than sneaking around as though we're doing something wrong? Not even able to tell my best friend or my family?'

Khalid stood there for a moment and watched the tears sliding down Emma's pale cheeks. Then he heaved a sigh and turned to Beatrice.

'You would really do this?'

Beatrice smiled, anticipating her revenge. 'Absolutely.'

CHAPTER THREE

BEATRICE put a lot of effort into her choice of outfit for her second meeting with Tariq Al Kamal. She was rewarded for her efforts by Khalid's look of total horror at the lime-green and orange Lycra mini-dress she had squeezed her voluptuous curves into during their plane journey.

'You're not seriously going like that?'

'I was aiming for tacky and tasteless.' Maybe, she conceded, catching her own reflection, she had gone too far.

'You achieved it,' Khalid promised, lifting his eyes from the exposed upper slopes of her breasts and wiping the beads of sweat from his brow.

'Thank you. I'm just hoping I don't fall off the heels,' Beatrice admitted.

'This is never going to work,' Khalid groaned suddenly.

'Not if you go into it with such a defeatist attitude,' Beatrice agreed. 'Look, if we're going to do this we're going to have to do it properly.'

She had spent most of their journey bolstering Khalid's flagging resolve, and this fresh crisis of confidence when her own nerves were jangling was not what she needed. She controlled her impulse to tell him to show a little backbone and forced a coaxing smile.

'I know you think this brother of yours is omnipotent, or something.'

In Beatrice's opinion he was nothing but a control-freak

bully, and she was looking forward to taking him down a peg or two.

'But the fact is *he* was the one who thought we were an item…' She was encouraged to see Khalid smile.

'Is it always this hot?' she asked, flexing her shoulderblades to ease the clingy cloth of her dress away from her sticky skin as they crossed to the waiting helicopter.

The heat had hit her like a solid wall as they had left the air-conditioned comfort of the private jet with the royal logo emblazoned on its wings.

'No, there's usually a breeze from the mountains. Bea, are you sure you want to do this?' Khalid asked suddenly.

Beatrice wasn't, but she knew it was too late to turn back now. 'I'm looking forward to giving your brother a headache. I was actually wondering if there are any other male relatives other than him I can try and seduce.'

Khalid's expression grew seriously worried. 'Look, Bea, I know you think this is some sort of joke, but you can't play games with Tariq. You'll get hurt.'

'I really don't know why you're so afraid of this man.'

'I'm not afraid of him,' Khalid protested. 'He's actually a great person, and I can't tell you how many times he's bailed me out of trouble,' he admitted, looking sheepish. 'It's just when he decides something…' He shrugged. 'Well, you should under-stand— you've got some pretty strong views too.'

'Are you saying I'm like your brother?' Beatrice was appalled at the suggestion she bore any similarity to him.

Khalid grinned. 'No, you're much prettier. Now, have you been in a helicopter before?' he asked as they reached their waiting transport.

'Never, but I'm always up for a challenge.'

As the helicopter hovered Khalid pointed out the cave homes carved into the same red rockface from which the royal palace rose. It was magnificent, and looked like something a special effects artist had created, Bea thought.

'They were actually lived in as recently as the sixties,' he said.

Bea gave up trying not to be impressed.

'Now,' Khalid explained, 'they are preserved—like a sort of museum.'

'For the tourists?'

'Tariq,' he told her earnestly. 'He thinks it is important to remember where we come from.'

For a split second she felt a stab of envy. It must be nice to know exactly where you came from, to have a place and people you identified with—to have roots. Then she pushed aside the wistful thought. She might not have roots, but at least she had her freedom, and no brother telling her how to live her life.

This wasn't the first time Khalid had quoted his brother. It seemed to Beatrice that the biggest favour she could do Khalid was to get him out from under his brother's thumb—though maybe it might not be as easy as she had first thought. It was never easy to break the habit of a lifetime, and thinking his brother's opinion on any subject was the definitive one was clearly not a recent development.

There was an air-conditioned limo waiting to whisk them the short distance inside the walls of the palace compound, and Beatrice welcomed the luxury and brief respite from the heat.

'Sir...'

The deferential manner everyone here adopted towards Khalid was going to take a bit of getting used to, Beatrice decided as she waited for this man to finish talking. She didn't understand a word that was being said, though the manner of both the man and Khalid suggested urgency.

'Is something wrong?' she asked, when the older man bowed low and vanished down the long marble-floored corridor, which resembled the several other marble-floored corridors they had already walked along.

'I'm afraid so,' Khalid admitted with a rueful grimace. 'There's a problem with the new irrigation project up in the southern desert and they need me. Tariq is waiting.'

Beatrice placed a soothing hand on his shoulder. 'Go, Khalid—I'll be fine.' Lost, but fine, she thought, looking down the seemingly endless corridor.

'Really?' Khalid smiled his gratitude. Still he hesitated. 'I hate to leave you like this.'

'Will you go?' Beatrice gave him a playful push just as a young woman appeared. Like the other women she had seen in the compound, she wore her hair covered but had no veil, and, like those other women, this one stared in fascination at Bea's fiery hair.

'Azil, here, will show you to your rooms. I'll be as quick as I can, I promise.'

The sweet-faced girl, her big doe-like eyes encircled by kohl, smiled shyly at Bea and began to walk down the corridor. Beatrice struggled after her in the unfamiliar heels. She felt that wearing her usual uniform of sneakers, jeans and T-shirt would have failed utterly to convince the awful brother that she had what it took to enslave anyone, let alone a member of royalty!

'Could you hold on a moment? These things are killing me.'

'Pardon?'

Rolling her eyes, Bea pointed down at her feet. 'The shoes—I have to take them off.'

The girl watched in astonishment as Bea removed first one spindly-heeled shoe and then the other. Then, as Bea wriggled her toes and sighed with bliss, she giggled.

She was still giggling when a shadow fell across them.

Bea turned her head, the shoes dangling from her fingers falling noisily to the floor. She did not need the girl's sudden deferential manner to tell her who was standing there. All the hairs on the nape of her neck were standing up in warning.

He said something to Azil that caused her to bow her head and hurry away.

Bea felt a strong desire to follow her.

Tariq turned slowly. The last time they had met, her face had been bare of make-up, but now she had plastered it on liberally.

The outfit she wore was simply outrageous, and was so obvious it was almost amusing.

But he didn't laugh. It would be a mistake to underestimate her. He had seen the sinuous, overtly sexual way she had moved as he had watched her and Khalid cross the courtyard together from the tower room. He did take some encouragement from the fact they had not behaved like lovers who could not keep their hands off each other—in fact they had not touched at all.

Had there been a lovers' tiff? Had seeing this woman in his home environment made his brother appreciate how ludicrous such a liaison was?

As their eyes connected Beatrice felt a wave of heavy inertia wash over her.

In a suit, Tariq had looked incredible, but with the dusty heels of his riding boots visible beneath flowing desert robes, and his face framed by a guttrah, he looked like nothing she'd ever seen outside her most unrealistic fantasy.

Beatrice closed her open mouth and prodded her antagonism into life. Of course he isn't like any male you've ever seen, Bea. He looks as if he's just walked out of a Bedouin tent.

For some reason she'd been expecting him to be dressed in Western attire, and she hadn't been mentally prepared for the sort of rampant sexuality he radiated.

Calm down, Bea. Underneath the outfit he's just a man like any other—except for his inflated opinion of his own importance and his unlimited reserves of money.

She responded to her own advice and lifted her chin—she'd die before she'd let him see how intimidated she felt.

I'm calm and I'm in control, she told herself as he moved a step closer with a fluid grace that made her stomach muscles clench and quiver in a disconcerting way.

She looked at him and reminded herself that this was the man who was out to ruin the lives of her friends.

Only she wasn't going to let him.

She took a deep breath that had an unfortunate effect on the too-tight bodice of her dress. Despite the heat a rash of goose-

bumps erupted under her skin, and her scalp tingled as she
absorbed the chiselled planes and contours of Tariq Al Kamal's
amazing face.

Beatrice knew he was half-English, but there was very little
hint in his face of his European heritage. His cleanshaven jaw
was angular, and his strongly defined razor-edged cheekbones
echoed the primitive sybaritic quality suggested by the curve
of his sensually sculpted lips.

He was the most beautiful man she had ever seen.

'I thought you were waiting for Khalid.'

'I am going to join my brother shortly.'

'Gosh, you take your duties as host very seriously. I'm
touched.'

He did not respond to her gushing insincerity. 'If you are not
here when we return I will double my initial offer.'

'Tempting,' she drawled, dredging up a smile from somewhere. 'But, you know, now I see the place it's like I said. I
rather fancy myself as a princess. It's every little girl's dream,
you know.'

'You are not a little girl,' he said, looking at her cleavage. 'I
also wonder if Khalid realises you're the sort of woman who
runs to fat.'

'I doubt it. One of life's great innocents—that's our Khalid.
He thinks you're a great guy.'

His eyes narrowed. 'If you felt anything for my brother,
Miss Devlin,' he hissed, 'you would not marry him.'

It was difficult not to contrast his manner unfavourably with
Khalid's self-deprecating humour.

She gave a mental shrug. Arrogance was pretty much a
prerequisite for someone in his position—someone raised
and brought up with the knowledge that he would one day be
King.

No wonder, really, she conceded, that arrogance and hauteur
were imprinted in every angle and hollow of this man's sculpted
symmetrical features.

She had never been in the presence of someone who exuded
a tangible physical charge before. It was extraordinary, almost

electrical, she thought, rubbing the tingling flesh on her bare arms and glaring at him.

His eyes dropped once more to her heaving bosom, and Beatrice struggled with the defensive impulse that made her want to cover what suddenly felt like acres of exposed flesh with her hands.

Instead she stuck out her chin and her chest and summoned a brilliant and patently false smile.

'And call me Bea. After all,' she said, shooting Tariq a flirtatious look from under the sweep of her lashes, 'I'm almost family.'

He gave her a look that said, as clearly as a siren, *Over my dead body*, and gave her a smile as false as her own. His heavy-lidded and extravagantly lashed eyes shone with overt scorn as he murmured, 'Miss Devlin, you will never be family.'

Beatrice swallowed the bubble of anger and reminded herself that this was the reaction she had wanted as she watched him stalk down the corridor, his white robes billowing around him.

Her own reaction as those dark eyes had moved insolently over her body was less desired. Awareness still tingled along her nerve-endings.

'Miss…?' the girl Azil held out the shoes to her.

Beatrice smiled and took them, casting one last look over her shoulder at the tall retreating figure. So confrontations with him were not easy on her nerves…imagine what stuff like that would do to gentle Emma!

CHAPTER FOUR

THREE days later Beatrice knew her suite and a small section of the palace rather well.

She had received exactly two telephone messages from Khalid. Both had been vague about when he'd return. In both he'd hoped she was being looked after.

She had to admit she *was* being looked after. She was sleeping in the most luxurious room imaginable, she was being waited on hand and foot, and the food was so good she was pretty sure she had already gained five pounds!

They treated her like an honoured guest, but Beatrice felt in all but name like a prisoner in a rather beautiful cage. She knew from Khalid that several members of the royal family had rooms in the palace compound, but she had been introduced to none, remaining totally segregated.

It was subtly done of course—a locked gate or door, a polite 'this area is private'—but she nevertheless knew her movements were being monitored and restricted. She hadn't tested these restrictions yet, but that was about to change.

Her mouth firmed as she tied the headscarf supplied by helpful Azil over her bright red hair and tucked in a few stray curls. Then she checked out the long skirt and kaftan top she had selected in the full-length mirror.

She gave her reflection a nod of approval, opened the door of the luxurious apartment and smiled sunnily at the man standing outside.

'Good morning, Sayed.'

The thickset man dressed in traditional desert garb bowed his head courteously. Though there were others, this older man was her shadow—or jailer, depending on your point of view. She had the impression from the way he was treated that his position in the household was not as humble as he would have liked her to think.

'I'm going out today.'

For once his impassive expression faltered. 'Out?' he said uneasily.

She nodded cheerfully. 'Into the city. I feel like exploring.'

'I don't think that is a very good idea, miss...'

'When he comes back I'll tell your boss. I'm assuming you report back to the Crown Prince direct?'

There was a pause before the other man swept her a low bow. 'That is so, Miss Devlin.'

'Right, I'll tell him you did your utmost to dissuade me but I took no notice. Would you call me a taxi?'

'I really don't think...'

'Of course my friend in the British Embassy would be perfectly willing to pick me up if you're too busy,' she said, amazing herself with her powers of invention. 'I hate to ask him as he's always sorting out some diplomatic incident or other, and you know what a pain that is, but he's always said if I'm ever in town...'

'I will order a car, miss...'

Beatrice, who had been holding her breath, heaved a sigh of relief as the traditionally garbed figure vanished to make whatever arrangements he deemed necessary. Smiling, she chalked up an invisible point in the air. Of course she might have been in trouble if he'd called her bluff...but she wasn't going to dwell on that.

Beatrice had no real idea what Tariq Al Kamal the royal pain in the neck intended to achieve by this enforced separation, but she had absolutely no doubt that it was his doing.

She wouldn't put it past him to deliberately sabotage the irrigation scheme himself, in order to remove his brother from her evil influence! He was probably even now drip-feeding Khalid more poison about her—the irony being that Khalid undoubtedly agreed with his brother concerning her total unsuitability for the role of royal consort.

Presumably Tariq imagined this period of isolation—a stranger in a very strange land scenario—would make Bea more malleable and more inclined to accept whatever bribe or threat he was going to offer her when they returned.

If so, his plan had backfired. Beatrice did feel isolated, out of place and lonely, but she also felt mad as hell at being manipulated this way. It might be hard, but she was determined to live up to Tariq's expectations of her if it killed her.

She smiled in anticipation of seeing the supercilious snake squirm.

After the open spaces and tranquil silence of the palace the noise, sheer vibrancy and buzz of the capital stunned Beatrice to silence.

The limousine Sayed had produced made her feel like a modern-day Cinderella—though obviously minus the Prince. Now, as they drove down the wide, tree-lined boulevards of the modern part of the city, he gave her a running commentary on points of interest.

She listened politely, but he was giving her information she'd already read when she had done her research. She knew that Zarhat was politically stable, culturally diverse, and had an economy that was the envy of its neighbours. She knew the people were incredibly loyal to the royal family, and that they enjoyed a very high standard of living. She knew that over the past thirty years the country had reclaimed thousands of acres of desert and that agriculture thrived. In short, many considered Zarhat a model country.

'I'd like to see the old city.'

'The streets and alleys are narrow, and it would be difficult to take the car…'

'I'd much prefer to walk.'

Sayed took a little persuading, but he came round when he saw she was determined.

'Sayed?'

The older man bowed his head respectfully to the Crown Prince.

'What is this?' Tariq pointed at the large box of elaborately decorated sticky sweetmeats on his desk and gave a grimace of distaste. 'I don't have a sweet tooth.'

'I'm sorry, sir, they shouldn't be here. They're for Miss Devlin, from the Rajoub family.'

Even her name conjured an image of her lush lips parting under the pressure of his. She would taste— The silence was punctuated by the sound of the pencil he held between his fingers snapping.

Conscious it was his brother who ought to be displaying the classic signs of sexual frustration and not him, Tariq glared accusingly at Sayed. 'Miss Devlin…?'

'Yes, they arrive for her every day. She does have a sweet tooth, but she gives most of them away to Azil, who has many sisters.'

Tariq's brows lifted. Sayed was smiling. He had never seen Sayed smile before, and it was a bit like seeing a granite rockface suddenly grin—slightly unnerving.

'Why are the…Rajoubs…?'

'Yes, sir—the Rajoubs. They are a very respectable family. They have a small shop on the—'

Unable to conceal his impatience, Tariq cut across the older man. 'Why is this respectable family sending Miss Devlin cakes?'

'They feel grateful after she saved the little boy.'

Tariq sat down and lifted a hand to his head. It wasn't aching yet, but he felt it was probably only a matter of time. 'I think, Sayed, that you had better start at the beginning.'

He managed to stay silent until Sayed had finished.

'So, to summarise, you allowed Miss Devlin to leave the palace?'

'I did not have the authority to stop her, and I wanted to avoid a diplomatic incident...'

'Diplomatic...?' Tariq shook his head, 'No, don't tell me. I'm still trying to unravel the facts I have. You allowed her to wander around the streets...' He could imagine what havoc her red hair and smiles had created.

'I was with her.'

Tariq brushed aside the defence. 'To wander around the streets, throw herself in front of moving traffic to save a child, and become lifelong friends with his entire family?'

'Yes.'

'Yes? Is that all you have to say?'

'She is a very friendly young lady, sir, and very quick-witted.'

Tariq stared at the older man. It seemed impossible, but was that a note of reproach in Sayed's voice...?

He had returned expecting to find at best that the woman had got the message, given up and gone home, at worst that she would be here, but considerably subdued by her lonely wait.

Now it seemed she had been busy rushing around the city playing heroine, and making the most loyal and trusted members of his household fall under her spell!

'I suppose my father has invited her to dinner while I was away?'

Sayed responded seriously to the sarcasm. 'The King has not left his apartments.'

Tariq nodded. The King had not left his apartments for two years, but that was not a concern he could deal with now. Now it seemed wise to focus on the Beatrice Devlin problem. He had clearly underestimated his adversary.

'Right, Sayed—do you think you can relay a message to Miss Devlin for me?'

Sayed bowed his head.

'Ask her to meet my brother at the pool in half an hour.'

'I did not know that Prince Khalid had returned.'

'He hasn't. And, Sayed...?'

'Yes, sir.'

'Will you please take that disapproving look off your face?'

CHAPTER FIVE

WHEN Beatrice finally located the indoor pool Khalid was already in the water, swimming with a rhythmic strength that suggested he was a lot fitter than she had ever thought.

She slipped off her sandals and looked around. Khalid, unaware of her presence, continued to swim up and down the Olympic-sized pool with metronomically precise strokes, barely causing a ripple in the water. As she watched he reached the far end, where a waterfall tumbled into the water, and, barely pausing, flipped over like a seal and continued.

Impressive!

Almost as impressive as this place.

Beatrice tilted her head back to gaze in awe at the vaulted ceiling, stained glass alternated with moulded panels, richly decorated with vibrant golds and blues. The same colours were echoed in the mosaic underfoot. The palms and lush exotic vegetation that towered overhead looked startlingly green against the azure backdrop.

After a week in the royal palace she'd just about run out of superlatives.

Dropping her towel on a chair, she padded to the water's edge; the water looked incredibly inviting. Squatting down, she trailed her fingers in the water just as Khalid's fingers touched the edge.

'I'm impressed,' she admitted as his dark head lifted. The smile on Beatrice's lips faded dramatically as she found herself looking into sardonic silver-flecked dark eyes that did not belong to Khalid.

The teasing smile that had tugged her lips upwards evaporated, and she almost fell over in her haste to move away as the swimmer heaved himself out of the water in one supple motion.

Eyes wide and shocked, Beatrice watched as Tariq shook his head, sending a shower of droplets into the air, some of which struck her hot skin. Then he dug his fingers in his saturated sable hair and pushed it back from his face. His skin gleamed like beaten copper, his face glistening under the water droplets that appeared as tiny crystals on the ends of his long sooty eyelashes.

'S…sorry—I didn't know you…' Her voice trailed off, the hot colour rising up her neck as her eyes ignored all the frantic instructions coming from her brain. Her gaze flickered downwards and the breath snagged in her throat as a wave of heat washed over her fair skin.

It had always been obvious that Tariq was in pretty marvellous physical condition, but just how marvellous had been left to her wilful imagination. Now she knew her imagination had lagged way behind reality.

Whatever else Tariq was, he was totally magnificent! His body long and greyhound-lean, shoulders broad, chest and shoulders deeply muscled, his belly washboard-flat. He carried no excess flesh to blur or conceal the taut, perfectly muscled delineation of his body.

'Sorry—I didn't know…'

He arched a sardonic brow and it was a moment before she could retrieve her line of thought.

'I th…thought…'

You're not here to act like a blushing virgin with a crush, Bea. Just pull yourself together. He's got a body—it's not as if you didn't already know.

She took a deep sustaining breath and counted silently to ten before she spoke again.

'I was meant to meet Khalid. He…' Her voice trailed to a

whisper as things inside her quivered. His black swim shorts had slipped an inch to reveal a thin line of skin a paler shade of gold than the rest of his torso. For some reason she couldn't take her eyes from that narrow strip of skin, or the fine line of dark hair that vanished like a directional arrow under the waistband.

'I sent the message.'

'You did?' Trying to kick-start her brain, which was like trying to think through cotton wool, Beatrice dragged her eyes back to his face.

'Are you not going to swim? You look as if you could do with cooling down.'

Beatrice's chin came up with a snap. As her gaze clashed with his mocking stare she felt her temper fizz into life—the man knew exactly what he was doing to her, she thought furiously. But then he would, wouldn't he? He'd probably been turning women into drooling idiots all his adult life.

Fortunately she was not about to lose her objectivity and her focus just because he was one of those men who projected a sexual aura. *Like you've met so many, Bea!*

'For a self-confessed gold-digger you blush awfully easily,' he observed, his voice harsh.

Did she cultivate the habit to make men feel more tender and protective towards her? he wondered cynically.

Biting her lip and cursing her fair skin, and the childish habit she had never grown out of, Beatrice lifted a hand to her burning cheek.

'I'm not used to the heat.'

'Don't get any idea you'll have time to acclimatise...'

'If you're not careful I might get the idea you don't like me.' Beatrice smiled, pleased when he responded to her provocative pout with a heavy frown.

'You are not the sort of woman that men *like*; you're the sort of woman that men want. But, as you must know, the novelty soon wears off.'

The insult was as calculated as the sneer that tugged the corner of his mobile lips upwards, and her eyes sparkled with anger.

'And do *you* want me?' The moment the words were out of her mouth Beatrice wished them unsaid. The air between them crackled with a sexual tension that hung heavy between them.

One dark brow elevated to a satirical angle. 'Is that an invitation?'

The heat flared even hotter in her cheeks. 'I already have a lover.'

The reminder caused anger to flash like a silver flame in his spectacular eyes. 'He's not here,' he reminded her.

'But he's worth ten of you! And I didn't say I was a gold-digger, you did—which was a judgement you made even before you met me, you smug, sanctimonious bully!'

His incredulous intake of breath was audible. 'You dare speak to me in this manner?'

Beatrice gave a shrug, calculated to aggravate this self-important Prince and disguise the illicit shudder of excitement that had rippled through her body. 'Looks like it, doesn't it? What are you going to do? Throw me in jail…?'

A secure mental facility, she decided, might be more appropriate for a person who got a thrill from goading a man this dangerous!

'Do not tempt me,' he advised grimly.

'And, just for the record, it wasn't an offer.' She flicked him with a look of icy contempt and added, as much to convince herself as him, 'I wouldn't touch you if you were the last man alive!'

Tariq's gaze drifted from her stormy face downwards, over her body concealed in the billowing floaty folds of an ankle-length robe, and he found himself wondering how far the rosy glow on her translucent skin extended. Did that pink encompass all her soft pale curves and every inch of her silky skin?

There was a very simple way to discover the answer. They were close enough for her perfume to tease his nostrils, close enough for him to reach out and tug the tie at her waist, pull the gown off her shoulders and—

Beatrice stepped back, startled, when without warning he

turned and dived back into the pool, his entry so smooth there was no splash, just a slow, spreading ripple across the water and then nothing...

Tariq reached the bottom of the pool before he began to swim, skimming the tiled floor as he headed towards the opposite end of the Olympic-length pool.

His actions had not been inspired by a desire for exercise but by an urgent need to cool off in a way he had not experienced since he was a teenager. It had been jump in the pool or grab the woman and find out how she would taste by letting his tongue sink between those sinfully provocative lips.

His lack of discrimination and control disgusted Tariq. Khalid, he reflected grimly, would not have stood a chance against this woman!

The thought should have made him feel sympathy for his smitten, lovesick brother, but as he thought of Khalid's hands on that lush body, his mouth on those lips, the physical temptation his little brother had succumbed to and enjoyed, he felt no tug of empathy. Instead he experienced a shameful and irrational rage.

He swam until his lungs burned and then kicked for the surface. Even the cool water and his oxygen-hungry lungs had not totally extinguished the lustful ache in his groin.

'Did you hear me? The last man alive!' Beatrice had yelled at the spreading ripple in the water.

Stringing together a series of colourful insults, she began to pace the floor at the pool's edge, waiting for him to come up so that she could tell him exactly what she thought of him.

Only he didn't.

Could a person stay down that long? Or had he...? She shook her head, dismissing the creeping concern as ludicrous. The wretched man was probably doing it deliberately—trying to spook her.

And it was working. With each passing second her anxiety increased. There was total silence in the pool-room—besides the rasping sigh of her own breathing and the faint hum of the filtration system.

Get a grip, Bea, she told herself. You're letting your imagination get the better of you.

Any second now his dark head was going to break the surface, and she was going to tell him exactly what she thought of him.

People drowned in pools every day of the week.

Not people as fit as Tariq.

All the same… She dropped down on her knees, peering into the water, but the glare from the sun made it impossible for her to see beneath the mirrored blue surface.

She leapt to her feet, genuine fear in her face as she fought her way out of the ankle-length kaftan she had put on over her bikini.

She was an adequate rather than accomplished swimmer, and Beatrice's dive into the pool was not the thing of beauty Tariq's had been. Having swallowed water when she hit the surface, it took her a few moments and several gasps to fill her lungs before she swam in the general direction of the spot where he had vanished beneath the water.

Tariq surfaced at the far end and hauled himself from the water. He pulled his hand through his dark hair again and scanned the room with narrowed eyes. It was empty. Beatrice was gone. The groove above his masterful nose deepened. She hadn't struck him as the type who would duck a fight, or flee at the first sign of opposition.

Conscious of an irrational sense of anticlimax, he picked up a towel from a pile on a chair and headed for the changing room.

He had taken a couple of steps when she broke the surface, gasping. Between splutters, she began screaming for help.

It took him seconds to reach her.

'Relax!' he instructed tersely when she began to struggle, lashing out wildly as he slipped an arm across her chest. 'Don't fight me, you little fool,' he said, taking her face between his hands. 'You'll drown us both.'

Beatrice, breathless and exhausted, looked at him and then did something that surprised them both. She burst into tears and wrapped her arms around him, hiding her face in his neck.

'You're alive,' she said, her voice muffled by her tears and his damp skin.

'Not for much longer if you don't let go.' He was very conscious of her female curves insinuated against him, the smooth silkiness of her wet skin where it made contact with his. Her body plastered to his felt warm and soft, the essence of femininity.

Beatrice, too relieved to be embarrassed, took her hands from around his neck, feeling an odd reluctance as she did so. Then, expelling a long, shuddering sigh, she lifted her head from his shoulder.

Tariq's arms remained around her ribcage, supporting her weight in the water. Their faces were level as she looked at him, her wide emerald eyes swimming. Through the mist she didn't see the expression of something akin to shock that chased across his lean features.

The water had plastered her hair to her face and washed all trace of her make-up away, barring a dark rim around her eyes which made them appear enormous. Minus the make-up and the attitude, she looked very much younger and very vulnerable.

The misplaced tenderness he was shocked to feel stir inside him brought another harsh frown to his broad brow, and he clenched the fingers he had been about to smooth the strands of hair from her face with. This was the last woman in the world who needed protecting!

'Are you an imbecile? What did you think you were doing? If I hadn't been here...'

Beatrice's relief that he was alive vanished the moment she digested his harsh comment. For sheer irrationality he took first prize!

'If you hadn't been here I wouldn't have been trying to save you. Searching the bottom of a pool is not actually my idea of a good time.'

'You were trying to save me?'

The flash of his white teeth and his scornful laugh were like flames to dry tinder.

'Insane, I know!' she grunted as, hands flat on his chest, she tried to push him away.

She would have succeeded if the arm looped around her hadn't tightened like an iron band around her waist, securing her reluctantly to his side.

'But look at it from my point of view,' she said gritting her teeth and glaring at him. 'If you'd managed to kill yourself while you were playing "See How Long I Can Hold My Breath" they'd probably have charged me with homicide!'

'You're crying!' Amazement at this discovery could be heard in Tariq's voice as he watched the tears that seeped from her luminous eyes fall and mingle with the moisture already on her porcelain-smooth face.

'Don't worry—I'm not about to fall apart, despite the provocation. I always cry when I'm mad.' And this man seemed capable of making her madder than anyone she had ever met.

'I'm guessing Khalid has never heard you shriek,' he said with a grimace.

The grimace was more connected to the effort it took for him to wrench his eyes from her heaving bosom than the damage to his eardrums. 'Are you always this irrational and emotional?' Maybe only when she was slippery and wet? And half naked. But he was actually trying hard not to think about that.

'Pardon me if I come ever so slightly unglued at the thought of dead people—even you.'

He gave a grunt that sounded almost like a laugh, though there was no humour evident in his expression as he sternly advised her to stop thrashing around.

'I'm quite capable,' she began, when she realised his intention of towing her to the side.

He silenced her with a look.

Beatrice struggled to hold the gaze of those pewter-flecked eyes. She even considered arguing, but decided on balance that discretion might be the more sensible alternative to valour, as she wasn't totally sure she was capable of getting to the side herself after all.

When they reached the side he reached down, put a hand under her foot and boosted her up. Floundering, and feeling about as elegant as a beached whale, Beatrice pulled herself onto the tiled surface and lay there, with her feet in the water and her cheek pressed against the tiled surface.

'Get up.'

She sensed him standing over her, opened one eye and said, 'Leave me alone. I've just had a near-death experience.'

With what she considered to be a heartless laugh, he snorted. 'Don't be so dramatic. You were never in any real danger.'

Beatrice, still breathing hard, rolled onto her back and squinted up at the dark outline of him looming over her. 'So you're the expert on near-death experiences?' She closed her eyes and muttered, 'I wish I'd let you drown.'

He knelt beside her as she lay there, her breasts heaving and her water-darkened hair spread about her, making her appear to him like some exotic flower. Her delicate blue-veined eyelids flickered and then lifted as her glance slid up over his body until it reached his face.

'So, you like what you see?'

'What can I say? You're just perfect...' she drawled, working on the theory that this was one of those occasions when the truth was the best form of defence.

And it *was* the truth. From the sinewy strength of his long, muscular, hair-roughened thighs, to his broad, perfectly proportioned shoulders, and including everything in between, his body was perfect.

'If I wasn't already spoken for...'

One corner of his mobile mouth curled sardonically. 'So you love my brother?'

She gritted her teeth and matched the silky sarcasm in his voice, then added some of her own. 'More than life itself.'

He laughed, throwing Beatrice off balance—he looked so sinfully attractive. She snarled scornfully. 'At least I'm not as cynical and twisted as you are. And where,' she demanded, struggling to keep the panic from her voice, 'is Khalid, you lying rat?'

From the look of astonishment that moved across his face she was thinking the Crown Prince might not be used to being called a liar or a rat. Well, while she was around he might as well get used to it, she decided belligerently.

'I'm afraid that Khalid's presence is still required out at the irrigation project. He sent his apologies and his kisses…' he said, looking at her mouth.

Beatrice's eyes narrowed as her insides dissolved. 'Don't even think about it!' she warned, her lips tightening with anger as she pulled herself upright and brought her knees up to her chest. 'You probably invented the entire crisis!'

And I'm having one all of my own, she thought, trying and failing to stop her eyes filling with tears again. To display such weakness in front of this man filled her with horror—though he'd probably think any display of emotion from her was part of some act.

He appeared unperturbed by her accusation. 'The crisis is genuine, I can assure you.'

And probably one that his brother, with his degree in engineering, was better qualified to deal with than he was. Tariq had been favourably impressed by the way his little brother had handled himself. Maybe, he mused, it was time he encouraged Khalid to make more use of his qualifications and come home? He had definitely got the impression that the playboy lifestyle no longer exerted the same pull for his brother. Personally, the aimless existence would have bored him out of his skull in two seconds, but he and Khalid were very different people.

Though maybe they were attracted to the same sort of women. The difference was *he* was not a hopeless romantic.

'But I will not deny it is convenient, for now we can take off the gloves without fear of interruption.'

He wasn't wearing gloves. Beatrice was extremely conscious, as he was kneeling about six inches from her, that he was actually wearing very little. Her eyes slid to his hands, brown and shapely, with long tapering fingers—the sort of fingers that would know their way around a woman's body.

My body… A silent shiver started deep down inside her and rippled outwards until the conflicting emotions of heart-thudding fear and suffocating excitement blurred into one hunger.

The strength of the primal reaction shook Beatrice to the core and, both appalled and ashamed, she wrenched her gaze from his hands. Staring at the mosaic floor instead, she took a deep breath and struggled for control. Of course she knew that a lot of women would have dissolved like ice cream in the desert sun when faced with Tariq's primitive brand of raw sexuality, but the shock was to discover, after a period of successful self-denial, that she was one of them.

It was always useful to know your weaknesses, but actually this was an occasion when blissful ignorance would have been infinitely preferable. Not that she intended dwelling on it—after all, this wasn't about her, or her previously unsuspected weakness for arrogant, unreconstituted chauvinists with perfect bodies, and it had absolutely no bearing on why she was here.

This was about Emma and Khalid.

'Are you all right?'

The abrupt enquiry brought Beatrice's head up. Squinting, she lifted a hand to shade her eyes from a shaft of sunlight that fell directly on her face.

'Fine,' she lied, ignoring the apparent concern in his expression. Concern that would undoubtedly turn to smug amusement if he ever got an inkling of the effect he had on her hormones. 'Take off the gloves…?' she added with a scornful snort. 'Because up until now you've been so incredibly subtle?'

She took a hank of water-drenched hair and twisted it, allowing the excess moisture to pool on the ground before flicking it back over her shoulder. She lifted her eyes and her gaze brushed his, before dropping to the stern, sensual outline of his lips. Heaving a deep breath, she pushed away the images that threatened to invade her thoughts.

'Just what gives you the right to decide who your brother should or should not marry?'

He ignored the furious question the same way she suspected he would have liked to ignore her. Everything about her clearly offended him.

'What will it cost to make you give up Khalid?'

'I thought that wasn't open to negotiation? I must have got you worried.' She allowed him to see that the possibility she had got under his skin amused her. 'Or did your lawyers advise you to up the offer?'

'There are no lawyers here. Just you and I.'

The reminder was quite unnecessary. Beatrice could not have been more aware of the isolation of their position. 'Is that a threat?' she husked, sticking out her chin to show it hadn't worked...if only!

Tariq's sable brows lifted as he settled back on his heels, maintaining his squatting pose with no apparent difficulty. 'It is a fact.'

Beatrice swallowed and lowered her eyes; it amounted to pretty much the same thing from where she was sitting.

'I was simply saying that you can speak frankly.'

A laugh was wrenched from Beatrice. How wrong could a man be? Speaking frankly at that moment would get her into deep trouble.

'You probably have the place bugged.' She would put nothing, nothing at all, past this man, she thought wildly as he leaned closer, and her heart started to hammer even faster, as though it was trying to batter its way out of her chest.

'I offered you a lot of money, and presumably if that was all you wanted you would have taken it. So you want more than financial security for life? Is it the social position you want? The kudos of being the wife of a powerful man?'

'I hate to interrupt the great mind at work, but has it occurred to you that I'm simply in love?' she challenged, wondering how that would feel—to love a man as Emma loved Khalid?

Maybe she would never find out...maybe she was one of those people who were simply not capable of losing their hearts? And maybe that wasn't such a bad thing. After all, love hadn't brought poor Emma undiluted joy.

He threw back his head and laughed.

Beatrice clenched her teeth and eyed him with loathing cloaked behind a brilliantly insincere smile.

'I can see I can't fool you. Maybe I don't love Khalid,' she conceded, 'not the way you mean. But then how do you define love?'

'A very philosophical thought.'

'However,' she added, longing with a violence that was outside her nature to slap that supercilious, disdainful smirk off his face, 'I am very fond of him, and I think he will make a very... comfortable husband. He's rich, not too set in his ways...'

'You mean easily led?'

He looked furious, which to Beatrice's way of thinking was slightly unreasonable, considering she was obliging him by being exactly the sort of woman he had decided she was before he had even met her.

'He won't know he's being led. The trick,' she confided, with a smile that caused him to audibly grate his teeth, 'is making him think it was his idea anyway.'

'You expect me to believe you will be faithful?'

'I'll be discreet. I'll never embarrass Khalid.' A choking sound escaped Tariq's throat and she tilted him a look of innocent enquiry. 'I'm not a romantic. The fact is—and I'm sure you'll agree...'

She paused for a second, but he didn't take up her invitation to say anything. He actually looked ready to throttle her.

'Well, personally I don't think it's realistic to expect a person to be sexually satisfied by just one person.'

His lips curled in disgust, and there was grim sincerity in his voice as he informed her, 'You will *never* marry my brother. No matter what it takes, I will prevent this union.'

CHAPTER SIX

BEATRICE struggled not to recoil as a shiver of fear traced a shaky path down her spine. She had the distinct feeling that he meant what he said quite literally. She was beginning to realise that she was playing with a ruthless man who was capable of breaking the rules when they inconvenienced him—in fact he was able to rewrite them if he felt like it.

'Now, there's no need to get emotional about this,' she chided. 'You wanted me to be frank—aren't you being just a tad hypocritical?'

A hissing sound of astonished outrage escaped the barrier of his clenched teeth. 'I think you would be wise to take care in what you say to me. I am not at this moment...safe.'

Beatrice made a pretence of being mystified by his reaction. 'There's no need to get on your high horse. Are you trying to tell me that *you've* always been totally faithful to the ladies in your life?' She loosed a tinkling laugh. 'I don't think so.'

His features stiffened into a rigid mask of hauteur. 'You know nothing of me.'

'And I don't want to!' she flashed back, slipping out of character for a moment as she glared at him.

'When I marry I will respect my wife, and I will not humiliate her by being unfaithful,' he informed her coldly.

'How sweet. But maybe you haven't got a healthy sexual appetite. I have...'

It was about halfway through delivering her provocative retort that Bea knew she had gone too far. But she was already committed, and the words just kept coming—until he leaned across her, his arm brushing her breasts as he placed a finger under her chin. Her words died along with rational thought as her eyes collided with his hungry, burning gaze.

The most disturbing aspect of this situation was not the fear that filled her, but the exhilaration and excitement that raced like a flashfire through her blood as he took a hank of her hair in one hand and angled her face up to his.

'I have a healthy sexual appetite...' he rasped.

'Great...' Her nervous little laugh emerged as a choked gasp as she babbled. 'That is, I believe you. I'm sure you're as macho as hell, and...' Her eyes drifted to the sensual outline of his mouth and the words dried on her tongue.

In her head she could hear the thunderous wild pounding of her own pulse. Her limbs felt like cotton wool, not totally connected to the rest of her body, as he ran a finger down the curve of her cheek. The smouldering heat in his eyes sent her senses spinning out of control.

'I enjoy a skilled lover who knows how to please a man.'

The words shocked Beatrice back into sanity.

What the hell am I doing?

She held up her hands in an instinctive gesture of rejection and they were immediately trapped between their bodies as Tariq jerked her to him, his body half-covering hers, only his supportive elbow stopping him pressing down on her.

Her raw gasp of shock merged with a series of shaky gasps from her lungs. She tried and failed to inject a note of amusement into her voice as she said, 'I'm not going to please *you*.'

I wouldn't have the faintest idea where to start!

Her glance drifted to his mouth, and a voice in her head said, *But it might be fun learning.* Her green eyes widened with horror as she caught herself agreeing with this aberrant thought.

He smiled, his glittering eyes sweeping across her passion-flushed face. 'Then I shall please you.'

The throaty promise paralysed Beatrice with lust, and she

started to tremble as she struggled to control the scary and intoxicating wildness that was burning in her blood.

This isn't me. I don't do this.

But she was doing it, and what was more she wanted to do it—more than anything in her life before. She wanted to let go and let instinct take over. She wanted to respond to him. But she couldn't let herself. She had to stay in control.

Tariq's lashes lifted from the razor-sharp edges of his cheekbones as he looked into her passion-glazed eyes and confided huskily, 'This is something I enjoy…pleasing a woman.'

Beatrice laughed, clinging like a drowning person to the shreds of her cynicism. 'Because you're such a giving man…?' The retort lost a lot of its bite because of the breathy delivery.

Her eyes closed and a fractured sigh was drawn from somewhere deep inside her as he swept his hands slowly down the curve of her back until they came to rest on the firm, rounded contours of her bottom.

'You feel how much I want to give you?' he slurred.

'Tariq, you're…oh, goodness!' Beatrice groaned as her head fell forward onto his shoulder.

He looked down at her graceful supine figure, one hand thrown above her head, her hair spread about her flushed face. She was breathing fast and shallow, her full breasts straining against her bikini top, her nipples clearly outlined, straining against the sheer black fabric.

He could no longer hear the alarm bells in his head as he leaned across and pressed his open mouth to the pale smooth skin of her stomach. Her body arched and she loosed a feral cry as he ran his tongue up the gentle curve of her belly.

Anchoring her hips to the floor with his hands, Tariq continued to taste and tease the silky flesh, not stopping until he drew cries of raw pleasure from her.

When he finally arranged his body down beside her she was shaking, her entire body covered in a fine sheen of sweat. As he covered her mouth with his, thrusting deep into the warm, moist recesses, she wrapped her arms around his neck and met his invasion with her own tongue.

She threw one long shapely thigh across his hip and he held it there, stroking the smooth skin with his fingers until she was shaking like someone with a fever. As she responded to his every touch Tariq struggled to rein in his hunger. His frantic need to possess her was like nothing he had ever experienced.

Welcoming the sensual demands of his lips, Beatrice was in the grip of a reckless excitement. Every nerve-ending in her body was alive and screaming for more as she ran her hand down his chest. Her fingertips caught in the swirls of body hair and she felt his muscles contract sharply, whilst the muscles of his belly tightened as she slid her hand lower.

Without taking his mouth from hers, he took her hand and laid his own fingers to hers, palm to palm. Then he arched over her and pressed her arms to the floor—either side of her head.

How did a man who would have someone to put the toothpaste on his brush if he wanted come to have calluses on his hands? The question ceased to be important as she felt his sensitive fingers move to her breasts. A cry was torn from her throat as he rubbed her engorged nipple through the thin fabric of her bikini top, sending hot stabs of burning pleasure through her aching taut body.

Hunger licked his body and hardened his desire to the point of a pleasure that bordered on pain as he heard his name torn from her lips.

Beatrice's head was spinning as he bent and touched his mouth to the aching nipple of one breast and then the other.

She felt herself spiralling out of control and didn't care. 'Don't stop!' she begged as he raised himself up over her on one hand.

He didn't respond to the plea, but instead slid the narrows straps of her top down over her shoulders, exposing the quivering peaks of her full breasts.

Still holding her gaze, he took her face between his hands and lowered himself down until her bare breasts were brushing his hair-roughened chest. Then he kissed her—a deep, drowning kiss. A multitude of emotions churned inside her as she clung to him, but uppermost—quashing the guilt, fear and confusion—was the desperate need to give herself body and soul to this man.

It shouldn't have felt right, but it did.

At first Beatrice had no idea why he suddenly rolled off her, presenting his back to her. She reached for him, curling her fingers around his arm, then she heard him speak—and not to her.

She couldn't see Sayed, who must be standing in the doorway, because Tariq's body blocked him from her view, but she could hear him.

Mortified colour scored Beatrice's cheeks as she covered her bare breasts with her hands, her breath still coming in choppy, uneven bursts. She lay wishing with all her heart that she didn't know how he tasted, how he felt, how he smelt.

What have I done?

They did not speak for long.

When Tariq turned back her bikini top was in place and she sat huddled in her robe, with her knees drawn up to her chin.

'I have to go.'

Her expression wooden, she didn't look at him. She couldn't. A cocktail of shame, embarrassment and self-loathing churned inside her.

She tried to think of something to say, but could only think about how his mouth had felt on hers. She shrugged in a manner she hoped indicated she wasn't much bothered what he did.

Actually, everything he did bothered her deeply. She could count on one hand the number of thoughts she'd had since they'd first met that hadn't included him.

Why the fascination? she asked herself. Sure, he was an incredible-looking man, and his background was about as glamorous as it came, but it was more than that…much more.

Something twisted hard inside her as she watched covetously through her lashes as he walked away.

He paused and looked back. It seemed to Beatrice that he

was about to say something, but then he appeared to change his mind and carried on walking.

Beatrice didn't know how long she sat there, shivering and alone, before she returned to her room.

CHAPTER SEVEN

BACK in her suite of rooms, Beatrice showered, standing for a long time under the powerful jets. When she finally stepped out her skin was tingling, but the water hadn't washed away the disturbing, alien emotions that churned in her belly. Or her guilt.

She was deeply ashamed. It didn't matter what sort of spin she put on it, her behaviour had been pretty much that of a trollop.

'The good point,' she told her pale-faced reflection as she dragged a comb through her wet hair, 'is that he now thinks you're exactly the sort of woman he always did. I'm not only an avaricious gold-digger, I'm an avaricious gold-digger with nympho tendencies...'

It couldn't have worked out better if she'd planned it, Beatrice acknowledged. But the thought did not bring her any glow of satisfaction. She felt so horrified at the thought of what she had been about to do but for the interruption that her stomach muscles twisted.

She had no excuse. It wasn't as if she was particularly highly sexed, and it wasn't as if men—some rather nice—hadn't tried to disprove her own private opinion that she was actually a bit of a cold fish.

She had realised pretty much the moment she'd bought her first bra that there was something about the way she looked that made men assume that she was some sort of smouldering volcano, even when she gave them the cold shoulder.

An image flashed into her head, and her eyelashes brushed against her flushed cheeks as in her mind she saw Tariq's long brown fingers slide slowly up the pale skin of her thigh. Her eyes glazed as the memory gained ground, reawakening the fever in her blood and the breathless anticipation, causing things deep in her pelvis to tighten and twist…

With a groan, she dropped her head into her hands. The conflict raging inside it made her feel as though it was going to explode. What she needed was a cold shower…another one… and something for her headache.

She took a couple of aspirin and selected a pair of jeans and a white linen shirt from her limited wardrobe—two of the few items she had brought with her that she would normally wear. It seemed wise to tone down her act, because given recent events it seemed she had played it a little too well.

She was sliding her feet into a pair of leather ballet pumps when there was a knock on the door. Tariq walked in before she had a chance to respond. Maybe he thought he had the right? Maybe he thought they were going to take up where they left off?

And who could blame him? Shame rose like bile in Beatrice's throat. Tariq was only assuming what most men would, given the fact that she hadn't exactly beaten him off with a stick!

Beatrice struggled to rationalise her recent wanton behaviour. It felt like an erotic dream—though no dream *she* had ever experienced. Maybe what had happened had been inevitable? A natural consequence in a highly charged atmosphere where feelings were running high and the two people involved were wearing very few clothes? Coupled with the fact that one of those half-naked people had an overpowering masculinity, and the other…well, the other, she decided with disgust, was just a push-over! She had acted with no vestige of self-respect, and he had made it clear he had nothing but contempt for her.

Bringing the inner dialogue to an abrupt halt, Beatrice took a deep breath, hooked her thumbs in the belt loops of her jeans, and gave Tariq a cool smile. What mattered was making it clear to him that it wasn't going to happen again.

'I'd like you to leave.'

Under the composed smile, Beatrice struggled silently with a fear she was ashamed to acknowledge before she lifted her chin to a combative angle and forced herself to take a step towards him. Still the fear lingered that if he touched her, if she got close enough to feel the heat of his body, she'd just melt again.

For goodness' sake, woman, get a backbone and stop acting like you're a heroine in some Gothic romance. This is the twenty-first century—he's not about to recruit you for his harem!

'Now, I don't want to make a scene.' Actually, she was pretty sure she could scream blue murder and people around here would turn a deaf ear. 'But I will.'

Tariq ran a hand across his jaw. 'There has been an accident,' he told her bleakly.

As Tariq delivered the news to Beatrice he had to remind himself that it had been no accident that Khalid had been where he was. *He* had arranged that—arranged his brother's delayed return— which made him directly responsible.

The last words Khalid had said before they parted rang in his head.

'Tell Beatrice I'll be back soon. And, Tariq, leave her alone— she's really not as…tough as she seems.'

He had given the required promise, lying with no sense of shame. His motivation was pure, or so he had told himself, and the end justified the means.

His brother needed saving from Beatrice Devlin and he'd achieve that—no matter what the sacrifice. And was it such a big sacrifice to engineer a situation that ended with him burying himself deep in her silken softness…?

Khalid's welfare had certainly not been high on his list of priorities half an hour ago.

'An accident…?' Beatrice knew she sounded stupid, but her brain refused to translate what he was saying.

'At the irrigation scheme.'

She swallowed. 'Tell me.'

'There were injuries.' The biggest injury was to his moral

authority. While he had been making love to the woman his brother loved, Khalid had been lying fighting for his life.

The colour leached from Beatrice's skin. An image flashed in her head of Emma looking up at Khalid, adoration shining in her eyes… If anything happened to Khalid she wasn't sure how her friend would cope.

'Khalid?'

'He's been injured. Sit down,' he said abruptly, because the alternative seemed likely she would fall down.

Nobody, not even an Oscar-winning actress, could have simulated the distress she was displaying. Though she was clearly struggling for composure, she was leaking distress from every perfect pore.

The possibility—and now it seemed a probability—that she had genuine feelings of some sort for his brother was not something that Tariq had even considered to this point. And now he was forced to consider it he resented it.

While he believed Beatrice Devlin an avaricious gold-digger, Tariq had some justification for his machinations. But if she wasn't, and if his brother was actually the luckiest man alive, then what did that make *him*?

But Beatrice Devlin's feelings, or even those of his brother, were not the issue. Neither, he reminded himself grimly, was the ache of thwarted desire in his belly or the fact he felt as guilty as sin.

Beatrice ignored his suggestion to sit down. Not because it wasn't a good idea, but because everything he said sounded like a decree, and it was genetically coded into her brain to react negatively to orders and authority.

'He has been taken to the hospital…'

Relief flooded through her. 'Then he's alive?' she breathed, adding a shaky, 'Thank God!' Then her knees gave way, and she sank to the chair Tariq pulled up in time to stop her landing in an inelegant heap on the floor.

'My father is already on his way to the hospital. I must join him there.'

This would be the first time since his stroke that his father, the King, painfully self-conscious of his slurred speech and too proud to allow his people to see he needed the aid of a stick to walk, had left his private suite.

Khalid's accident had done what he Tariq had failed to do for the past two years. But Tariq was in no mood to appreciate the silver lining in this situation.

'But Khalid—he will be all right…?'

'I will let you know when we have more news.' Tariq scanned her face and was relieved to see a tinge of colour in her cheeks. 'I will have someone come and attend to you.'

'I don't need waiting on. I've been looking after myself for a long time.' Beatrice was anxious that he did not judge her normal behaviour on the last few minutes.

'And now you want my brother to look after you? I can see the attraction of that for a woman who has been forced to live off her own wits.'

The assumption brought a sparkle of annoyance to Beatrice's green eyes. Knees like jelly, she got to her feet. 'I suppose you do know your ideas are straight out of the ark? Maybe there are some women who would sacrifice their independence and freedom for security, but not me. I'm not looking for any man to take care of me.' Beatrice knew that the only person she could rely on was herself.

He looked startled by her forceful pronouncement. 'Then why marry?'

She responded without thinking. 'Marriage has never been part of my plan…' 'Plan' was actually too definite a term, but Beatrice had never pictured herself meeting anyone she would contemplate spending the rest of her life with. 'I'm not into compromise.' And it often seemed to her that that was what marriage was all about.

'Then you met Khalid?'

She flushed self-consciously and silently cursed her runaway tongue. 'Then I met Khalid,' she agreed, as her lashes swept down in a concealing curtain.

'I will keep you informed of his condition.'

'You're not leaving me here!' she exclaimed. 'I'm coming with you.'

He spun back, looking startled by the comment.

'That is quite inappropriate.'

Beatrice stuck out her chin in response to the frigid dismissal, but her belligerence was superficial. It was just dawning on her that, whether she liked it or not, Tariq's word was pretty much law around here, and if he chose not to allow her access to Khalid there was not a damn thing she could do about it.

Actually, if Tariq chose to put her on the first plane home there wasn't a damn thing she could do about it!

It was a pity she couldn't use the same excuse for her shameful response to his lovemaking.

Banishing the stream of erotic images that flickered across her mind, she struggled to keep the cool smile in place. 'I really don't give a damn for appropriate. I'm not about to sit here twiddling my thumbs, waiting for you to remember I exist.'

An expression she couldn't quite pin down flickered across his lean features. 'I will not forget you exist.'

He didn't tack on *unfortunately*, but it was clearly what he was thinking. Quite irrationally, Beatrice felt a stab of hurt.

'Khalid is hurt and I want to be there.' She *had* to be there—for Emma. Depending on what she found at the hospital, she would have to make a judgement whether to inform Emma right away or wait until Khalid was better…*if* Khalid got better…

Beatrice felt panic crowding in on her from all sides, robbing her of the ability to think clearly. Eyes squeezed tightly shut, she fought her way past the knot of dread like a cold stone in her belly.

She sucked in a deep, steadying breath. There was no point assuming the worst. Until she knew otherwise she would work on the assumption that Khalid would be fine.

She dragged an unsteady hand through her hair, tangling her fingers in the damp curls. Her eyes drifted open and she became belatedly aware that Tariq was staring at her, his expression inscrutable.

Their eyes connected, and Beatrice let her hand fall to her side.

She took a deep breath. There was a time, she decided, for pride—and this was not it. He was not a man who responded to demands and ultimatums, but maybe a little genuine grovelling would work.

CHAPTER EIGHT

'PLEASE?' The word emerged huskily as she spread her hands in a pacific gesture.

A muscle clenched in his lean cheek and she saw something flicker in the back of his obsidian eyes.

Hoping it indicated a softening of his attitude, she added, 'I need to come. I need to be there.'

For a moment she thought he was going to dismiss her request out of hand, and then, with a slight shrug of his shoulders, he inclined his dark head. She followed him, and to her utter relief Tariq didn't object.

He strode down the corridor, leading the way through a door hidden by a heavy curtain. Behind it was a spiral staircase that led directly onto one of the inner courtyards.

As they stepped out of the big double doors two bodyguards fell wordlessly into step behind them. Beatrice's thoughts were too occupied elsewhere to consider the strangeness of spending your life constantly being shadowed by men who were willing to give their own life for you. A brief sideways glance at Tariq's profile suggested he was similarly preoccupied.

The helicopter was waiting for them, and the moment they were on board it took off.

'How long will it take?'

'We will be at the hospital in five minutes,' he said, without lifting his eyes from the hand-held computer he held. He clearly did not wish to make conversation, but Beatrice couldn't keep quiet.

'Did they say anything about...?'

He turned his head, moved his glance from her clenched hands to her tense face. 'They said nothing more than I have already told you,' he lied—not out of compassion, or a desire to protect her from the truth, he told himself, but because he did not want to cope with any hysterical outbursts.

When he'd last spoken to the hospital his brother was being transferred to surgery. Speed, they had explained, in such a situation was paramount, in order to avoid any possible permanent brain damage.

Beatrice's fingers continued to restlessly tap the rhythm to a nameless tune that she couldn't get out of her head. 'How can you work at a time like this?' She envied him his monumental calm. 'He's your *brother.*'

Tariq, who had been staring at a blank screen, lifted his head. The expression she glimpsed briefly in his deepset eyes made it clear that his detachment was an illusion. 'Would you like me to rant and tear at my hair to prove I care?' he wondered conversationally.

Beatrice gave a self-reproachful grimace. 'Sorry. That was unfair.'

'And you are usually always scrupulously fair?' he mocked.

'I try to be, and I know you care,' she conceded. 'In your own way...'

He laid aside the computer. 'What *is* my way?' She hesitated and he said, 'Feel free to speak your mind.'

'An over-protective, manipulative, control-freak way.' She saw the shock register on his face and thought, Oh, he didn't mean *that* free. 'I talk too much when I'm nervous.'

His mouth twisted into a sardonic smile. 'This I had noticed.'

Seeing the smile, Beatrice was relieved he hadn't taken offence. Given how reliant she was on his goodwill, there seemed little point going out of her way to aggravate him. 'You did say speak my mind,' she reminded him, shifting restlessly in her seat. 'I keep thinking if only...'

'If only what?'

'I know this isn't my fault.' Logically at least this was true.

Tariq tensed. Did she think he needed reminding that it was *his* fault? Did she think he wasn't aware that he had sent his brother into danger?

'If I hadn't come here it wouldn't have happened.' *If I hadn't interfered and meddled because I always think I know what was best.* 'Khalid would not be lying in a hospital bed.'

'No, he'd be lying in your bed.' His glance drifted over her face, lingering on her inviting lips. *It is where any man would want to be*, he thought.

It is where I want to be.

Embarrassed, Beatrice looked away. The only man she had ever wanted to share a bed with was sitting a few feet away. The knowledge scared her witless.

What is happening to me?

'Only if he had the energy to negotiate three miles of corridors.'

'True love always finds a way.'

The harshness in his voice made Beatrice turn her head sharply to look at him.

'You really do care for Khalid, don't you?'

She responded to the abrupt question without thinking. 'Yes, of course.'

'And you see no conflict in professing to love a man and sleeping with his brother?'

'I didn't...' Blushing to the roots of her hair, she threw a mortified glance over her shoulder, in the direction of the stony-faced guards. Her voice dropped to an agonised whisper as she added, 'We didn't...'

'Technically speaking,' he inserted sardonically.

'And that was sex, not love. I don't even *like* you!'

'You flaunt your body, yet you blush like a virgin when I mention sex.'

'I'm a mass of contradictions. It's part of my irresistible attraction.' She felt the helicopter drop and gave a sigh of relief. 'We're here.'

* * *

'You lied,' she accused in a quivering voice when the door closed behind the doctor.

He shrugged, and didn't look disturbed at the accusation. 'If I had told you the truth and said that Khalid needed surgery to relieve pressure on his brain would it have made you feel better?'

'This isn't about making me feel better,' she retorted, struggling to contain her temper. 'It's about you deciding in a patronizing, paternalist way what I should know.' She dashed a tear from her cheek as the hypocrisy of her accusation struck her.

Didn't postponing telling Emma about the accident make her guilty of the same thing?

She chewed her lip, agonising over her decision. Was she doing the right thing, waiting?

'Here.'

She stared blankly at the handkerchief he held out to her, then took it and blew her nose noisily.

'Thank you,' she sniffed, adding, 'You really are the most unbelievably arrogant man.' And the most beautiful, she thought, her glance drifting to the sensual outline of his mouth. She looked away as her body temperature rose in response to an intense hormonal rush.

'It is part of my irresistible charm.'

Beatrice didn't respond to the teasing reminder of her earlier remark. His irresistibility was no joking matter to her. It was a shameful distraction!

'He's out of surgery now?'

Tariq and the doctor had spoken briefly, and though she had caught most of it she wanted to be sure she had the essential details correct.

Tariq nodded. 'Yes, and things went very well.'

'But they won't know for sure until he regains consciousness?'

Tariq nodded again, his eyes on Beatrice's face.

'Can I see him?'

'My father is with him at the moment. I will come and get you presently.'

It was half an hour later when Tariq returned. Beatrice, who had spent most of the interval pacing up and down, had just taken a seat when the tall, commanding figure walked in.

Tariq's brows lifted as she leapt to her feet. The woman was wound tighter than a spring. He met her wide, anxious eyes and responded to her unspoken questions in the same tone he used to soothe stressed horses.

'Nothing has changed.'

She relaxed slightly, but still regarded him warily. 'You're telling me the truth?'

A week earlier he would have been deeply affronted to have his truthfulness questioned, and Tariq stiffened. But he had almost grown to expect casual insults from Beatrice. As he read the genuine anxiety in her face, he relaxed, 'Don't go paranoid on me, Beatrice Devlin. Do you want to see Khalid or not?'

She nodded, and flashed him a smile of gratitude as she walked past him into the glass-walled corridor. There was a visible heavy security presence in the ultra-modern hospital that Beatrice assumed was because a high-ranking royal was a patient.

Outside Khalid's room, Tariq paused, his hand across the entrance to prevent her entering.

'There are tubes and bandages. Do not be alarmed by them.'

Beatrice was glad of the warning. Khalid, lying there with his head swathed in bandages and his face bruised, was a truly shocking sight. As she gazed at her unconscious friend, her face soft with compassion, another face superimposed itself momentarily over his…that of her mother. That last time Beatrice had seen Laura Devlin her body had been worn down by the disease that was killing her, and had barely been recognisable to her daughter.

Beatrice struggled to clear the image from her past, as that was not the way she liked to remember her mother. In the end it was the sound of Tariq's rough velvet voice that enabled her to push aside the bad memory.

'Are you all right, Beatrice?'

Aware of the comforting weight of his hand on her arm, she turned her head. She felt his fingers tighten on her arm as their glances connected, and Beatrice felt a strong compulsion to lean into him. She didn't know if she actually swayed, or if it just felt as if she had, but she felt she was being drawn by some external magnetic force towards him.

'I'm fine.' She forced the husky words from her constricted throat, wondering what he'd do if she laid her head on his shoulder. Would his arms close around her? Would he push his fingers into her hair?

He'd probably call out to the guards outside the door to rescue him. Not that he had seemed to want rescuing earlier...

Tariq searched her face and looked palpably unconvinced but he did lift his hand from her arm—a move Beatrice found herself worryingly ambivalent about.

She paused a moment longer to compose herself before walking to the bed.

Across the room, Tariq watched her bend over the bed, pinning the sweet-scented swathe of her hair back with her one hand as she pressed a tender kiss to his brother's cheek.

A nerve clenched in his lean cheek before he turned and without a word walked away.

To feel jealous of his brother at any time would be appalling but to feel jealous when that brother was fighting for his life... His face darkened with self-revulsion. Under such circumstance it was utterly inexcusable.

He was the one who preached duty to his brother, and yet he was the one who had come perilously close to forgetting his duty and his honour because of an overwhelming need...a mindless hunger to possess a woman. Desire flowed hotly in his veins every time he looked at her. Not even in his adolescence had he felt so little control.

Beatrice sat by the bed alone but for the doctors and nurse who appeared at intervals. She watched Khalid, willing hi eyes to open, but they didn't. Instead, after hours of vigil, while she wrestled with the twin dilemmas facing her, her own eyes closed.

It was after midnight when Tariq, the desert sand still clinging to his clothes, returned to the hospital. A doctor was emerging from his brother's room as he approached.

The man stopped when he saw Tariq, and bowed his head in polite acknowledgment. Tariq dismissed the courtesy with an impatient movement of his hand.

'How is my brother?'

'We would have contacted you if there had been any change, sir.'

Tariq's face tightened in frustration as he struggled not to take his anger out on this man who, along with his staff, was working around the clock to help Khalid.

'Can you do nothing?'

The other man gave an apologetic grimace and shook his head. 'All we can do is wait.'

'This hospital has every piece of advanced medical technology known to man, and the best-qualified people on the planet, and all we can do is wait?'

'All the indications are good,' the doctor murmured soothingly.

'I do not want to be placated, Doctor, I want—' He stopped and took a deep, steadying breath as the other man visibly recoiled from him.

Chastising himself for intimidating the man, he sucked in air through his flared nostrils and lifted the corners of his mouth into a stiff smile. 'I'm sorry, Doctor,' he said in a milder voice. 'I know that you are doing your best. I am just not good at sitting around doing nothing.'

Beatrice had called him a control freak, and maybe she wasn't so far out. He certainly did not enjoy the feeling of impotence.

The doctor, looking relieved, hastened to assure him that he understood totally.

'I will sit with my brother.'

'Of course.' As Tariq reached for the door, the other man cleared his throat to gain his attention. 'You might like to keep the noi—' He stopped and looked uncomfortable, his eyes dropping from Tariq's as he muttered something indistinguishable under his breath.

'I might like to what, Doctor?'

'Well, I just thought…the young lady…she is asleep.'

Tariq was startled. It had been six hours since he had left. 'Beatrice…Miss Devlin is still here?'

'She hasn't left your brother's side. Such devotion… and such beauty…' The older man shook his head in wordless admiration.

'Just so, Doctor.'

The medic flushed under the hard look his future king gave him, and hastily excused himself.

Tariq went quietly into the room that was illuminated by the spotlight above his brother's bed.

Khalid looked very much as he had done when he had last seen him—maybe worse. His right eye was so swollen it distorted his features. Numerous tubes still protruded from his brother's left hand, and his right hand lay on top of the white sheet. His fingers, stained with the remnants of blood still engrained into the skin, were entwined with paler, slender fingers curled over them.

Beatrice, seated in the chair pulled up to the bedside, was lying half-slumped over the bed, her face pressed into the sheet. Her lips slightly parted, she murmured restlessly in her sleep.

As Tariq stared, she turned her head on the sheet to reveal her profile to him.

Just looking at her sleeping face made him feel as though a hand had plunged into his chest and grabbed his heart; the purity of her beauty touched something deep inside him. The fierce wave of protectiveness that rose up inside him was like a tidal wave, swamping every vestige of logic and good sense.

She cried out in her sleep, thrashing out with the hand that was not clinging to Khalid, as if to ward off the nameless monsters that filled her troubled dreams.

Was he one of the monsters? It would be more surprising, he reflected grimly, if he wasn't.

She cried out again, a lost little sound that stabbed into his heart like a blade. Of its own volition his hand went to her shoulder, closing over delicate bone and soft flesh.

'Hush, it's all right.'

Bea's eyes blinked open, and they were filled with fear and confusion and a total lack of recognition as she looked up at him. Gradually the glazed expression in the emerald depths cleared, and he saw the exact moment she remembered where she was and why she was there.

'Oh, I fell asleep.' She shivered. 'I don't know how that happened. I'm sorry...'

Tariq's hand fell away as she pulled herself upright, wincing as her stiff muscles complained. He watched as she carefully unpeeled her fingers from those of his brother.

'There was someone here to take you home when you were ready.'

'I wanted to stay, and it isn't my home,' Beatrice reminded him as she reached for the jacket she had folded over the back of the chair earlier. She slipped her arms into it and lifted a hand to her face, feeling the creases imprinted on her cheek.

She knew it was really shallow to care at such a moment about how she looked, but Tariq looked so damned incredible... even though his face and clothes were covered in a fine layer of reddish dust.

'Where have you been?' she blurted, unable to keep the note of censure from her voice as she added, 'I was alone.'

Mortified, Beatrice wanted the floor to open up and swallow her the second the words left her lips—*like I haven't been alone and doing fine all my life, thank you very much!*

She steeled herself. Because there was no way he would resist the opportunity to deliver a withering retort. And while she would normally not duck a fight or even a slanging match, Beatrice didn't feel very emotionally robust at that moment.

But the retort did not come. Instead, when she looked at him through the shield of her lashes, Tariq looked almost defensive—which struck her as extremely peculiar.

'Riding.' *Running away, more like*, the critical voice in his head chided. 'When I have things to think about I find it easier to clear my mind in the desert.'

Beatrice found it easy to see him on a horse, riding through the desert. The mental image had such a pull, the fantasy figure in desert robes was so real, that she almost didn't catch his addition.

'The hospital could have contacted me if there was an emergency. I had my satellite phone.'

'The doctors and nurses have been in and out, but they won't tell me anything.'

He gave a fierce look and demanded, 'Were they rude?'

The question and his inexplicable manner confused her further. She could see that he might have put hostilities on hold for the duration, but surely that didn't extend to him being protective of her?

Beatrice had never brought out the protective instinct in men—she had never wanted to—but now for the first time she could see that maybe there were some occasions when it might not be entirely unpleasant to feel feminine and in need of male protection. Temporarily at least.

'Were they meant to be?' He didn't smile back, neither did his fierce expression soften, so she added, 'No, not rude—just busy.'

'I saw the consultant on the way in.'

'Did he say anything…?'

'No change, apparently,' he said, seeing the flare of fear in her eyes.

'What time is it?' she asked, only just registering the darkness outside. Up until that point she had been busy registering Tariq, and every detail of his appearance down to the way his hair curled on his nape. She knew that the sharp visual image she had in her mind would never lose its clarity; he was burned into her mind for ever.

'Past midnight. You should go and get some rest.'

She shook her head. His dark gaze made her uneasy, restless and uncomfortably aware, and yet she knew the moment he left the room she would be waiting for the moment he came back.

Which made about as much sense as wanting to put your fingers into a live socket! She just couldn't make any sense of her complex feelings—but then she'd never met the living, breathing embodiment of her dark fantasies before.

One of these days, when she was far away from here, she might try and work out why he exerted this strange but compelling fascination for her. She was working on the theory that there was something in the spicy, humid air.

'I've had some rest,' she reminded him, nodding to the imprint of her head on the smooth hospital bedclothes.

'Is this display of devotion meant to impress me?'

Anger surged through Beatrice. This was what came of relaxing her guard around this man.

Before she could respond he added, 'If so, relax; I'm already impressed.'

In the middle of sweeping her tangled hair back from her face, Beatrice froze, her anger morphing into wariness. 'You are?'

'I can see now that you have genuine feelings for my brother.'

She stared, struggling to interpret the odd note in his voice and to understand the strained expression on his lean face.

'I will speak to my father. But that will be, I am sure, a mere technicality.'

'I don't understand? You'll speak to him? Speak to him about what?'

'I will not stand in the way of your marriage. I give my blessing to your marriage to Khalid.'

Beatrice's jaw dropped. 'Blessing…?' she echoed, thinking, *This cannot be happening.*

He inclined his head in a curt nod. Beside his mouth a nerve jumped.

Her plan hadn't just backfired, it had gone supernova on her face! 'But you think I'll pollute the gene pool…'

The comment caused dull bands of colour to appear across the slashing angle of his cheekbones.

'I did not say that,' he protested stiffly. 'Or even think it.'

Beatrice got to her feet, pushing her fiery hair from her face with both hands. 'Why are you saying this?' she asked, a hint of desperation in her voice.

'A situation like this…' His dark eyes flickered briefly to the silent bandage-swathed figure lying in the hospital bed. 'It reminds a person of what is truly important in life.'

Of all the times for him to get human and discover what was important in life it had to be now…Beatrice stifled an inner groan.

She didn't flinch or try to pull back as he reached out and took her chin in his long fingers, tilting her face up to his. She looked him in the eyes and felt herself drowning in the deep-silver star-speckled depths.

The searing strength of the emotions inside her as she looked at him rolled over her like a giant wave. The ache of longing, the need to be with him, to give herself without boundary or condition, went bone-deep.

It went soul-deep.

Then it hit her in a shocking rush of comprehension. Emotion thickened in her throat as a tiny shocked gasp escaped her frozen vocal cords. She suddenly knew without any doubt that she was looking at the man who was the love of her life.

She'd always considered unrequited love a little pathetic. Now she knew it hurt like hell and was totally illogical.

'You are not constrained by moral millstones—'

If only that were true!

'—but that does not make you a bad person. You have spirit and strength and beauty…'

He thinks I'm beautiful.

'And, yes, you are the most unsuitable bride ever born.' The tender quirk of his lips firmed as he added, 'But you love my brother.' He swallowed, the muscles in brown throat working as he said, 'And he loves you. Perhaps your marriage will work, perhaps not,' he admitted harshly. 'But one brother a slave to duty and tradition in a family is enough.'

The acrid edge of bitterness in his voice made Beatrice wonder if he hadn't at some point in his life sacrificed his own happiness for what he perceived to be his duty.

'You might think differently about this tomorrow…'

'My feelings on this subject are not about to change.'

'But—'

'Are you two arguing?'

Beatrice and Tariq turned in unison to the figure in the bed.

'My head aches.'

'Khalid!' Beatrice cried, running to the bed.

Tariq went to the door and spoke to the men standing outside. In response to his words one went running down the corridor.

'He's asleep again, I think,' Beatrice said when Tariq joined her. 'But this means he's going to be all right, doesn't it?'

Tariq stood at the bottom of the bed, his dark face split into a grin. 'It looks like it.'

Their glances locked, and with a cry of sheer undiluted joy and relief Beatrice ran into the arms he held open. Tariq swung her off the ground as though she weighed nothing and twirled her around. Still laughing, Beatrice tilted her face to his as he set her back down. His head bent to hers and she leaned up to press her lips to his, the gesture a spontaneous expression of relief and joy.

Their lips had barely touched before she realised what she was doing, and drew back with a small gasp of alarm.

She tried to pull away, but as Tariq's fingers, splayed at the small of her back, tightened she stopped.

Their gazes meshed, and everything except her heartbeat seemed to slow. A raw whimper was torn from her throat. His dark eyes glowed with a need that made her insides disintegrate.

He lifted a hand and ran a finger along the curve of her mouth, as though fascinated by the cushiony softness. 'You're shaking.'

'So are you.' Beatrice could feel the tremors running through his lean body.

'You're beautiful.' The febrile predatory glitter in his heavy-lidded eyes made her dizzy. Anticipation made her stomach muscles quiver.

'So are you. I think...'

'Don't,' he slurred, fitting his mouth to hers.

He kissed her deeply, drawing her body up and into his, fitting her soft curves into his hard angles as he plundered the sweet inner softness of her mouth. Beatrice moaned into his mouth as she speared her fingers into his dark hair to pull him closer.

When his mouth lifted neither moved. They stood breathing hard, their lips close but not quite touching, until the sound of a person nosily clearing his throat in the doorway caused them to break apart.

'Good evening, Father.'

Beatrice, her face scarlet, turned to see the King, flanked by two uniformed guards, standing in the doorway.

CHAPTER NINE

HAKIM AL KAMAL was not the frail figure Beatrice had been expecting, but a robust-looking man with a head of dark hair streaked with silver. His cleanshaven face was surprisingly unlined, and his piercing dark gaze was very familiar. It was at that moment moving from her to Tariq.

'This isn't what it looks like,' she blurted.

The King's bushy brows lifted towards his hairline. 'Things rarely are.'

'This is Beatrice Devlin, Father.' Tariq didn't appear to be even faintly discomposed by his father's arrival.

Beatrice didn't know whether she ought to bow or curtsy. Given the option, she would have fallen through a large hole that would have magically opened at her feet.

The arrival of the medical team *en masse* saved her from having to make the choice. In seconds the room was full of people, and she took the opportunity to move surreptitiously towards the door.

She was congratulating herself on her escape when a voice behind her stopped her in her tracks.

'Running away?'

Beatrice carried on walking, but a moment later he fell in step with her. 'It was a bit crowded in there,' she said, without turning her head.

'I need to go back.'

She gave a negligent shrug. 'Go,' she said, thinking, *Please!* It was hard not to think about that kiss—and if she did she really wouldn't be able to hold it together—when the person who had done the kissing was standing a few inches away.

Tariq looked at her set profile, expelled an exasperated breath through his teeth, and caught her by the shoulder.

'Don't touch me!' she breathed, backing away, her eyes wide.

'Don't worry—I will explain the situation to my father.'

Beatrice stared, and wished that first he'd explain it to *her*. How had this happened to her?

'He will give his permission for you to marry Khalid.'

Back at her apartments in the palace, Beatrice made the call to Emma. When the other girl had stopped alternately weeping and asking Beatrice if she was sure Khalid was out of danger, she announced with unusual determination in her soft voice that she would catch the next flight there and would see Beatrice when she arrived.

Beatrice didn't tell her that she wouldn't be there.

Her continued presence here would serve no useful purpose except to confirm the painful truth. She was in love with Tariq, and when he discovered the full truth about her deception—as he surely would—he'd despise her even more than he already did. If that were possible.

It turned out there were no seats on the direct flight back to London until the next day. Beatrice appealed to the booking clerk, who worked out a tortuous route home via France later today. But she'd get there quicker, he said, if she waited until the next day, and it would be a ten-hour stop-over in Paris. Beatrice booked herself a ticket anyway.

A ten-hour wait in an airport was to her mind infinitely preferable to risking the chance of coming face to face with Tariq and blurting out goodness knew what. All she had to do was keep a low profile until this evening.

She was considering how best to do that when a round-eyed and excited Azil appeared to tell her the King had requested that Beatrice visit him.

She broke off when she saw Beatrice's half-full case and exclaimed in dismay, 'You're not leaving, miss?'

'Yes, I'm going home.' *Only I have no home.* She felt the sting of self-pitying tears in her eyes and reminded herself that was the way she liked it.

Her lifestyle had made her adaptable. It meant she could come somewhere totally alien and exotic—and you couldn't get much more alien or exotic than Zarhat—and fit in without getting emotionally attached to the place...or the people. Then off she went to her next little adventure.

'I *like* meeting new people and only being responsible for myself.'

She saw the young girl staring at her in total incomprehension and thought, Who are you trying to convince, Bea?

'Ask Sayed to come in, Azil. I think you might have got the message wrong.' She had been here long enough to know that the King did not request visits from just anyone these days.

He communicated even with his most trusted advisors through Tariq, and until she had seen him today at the hospital Beatrice had imagined he was an invalid.

Sayed came in without an invitation, projecting disapproval.

'Does Prince Tariq know you are planning to leave?'

'Why should he? It's none of his business,' Beatrice retorted, sticking out her chin.

'I think it is possible he might not agree with you.'

So, nothing new there! 'Your Prince,' she said slamming down the lid, 'thinks *everything* is his business. Azil has been telling me the King wants to see me. I'm assuming she's got that wrong.'

'His Highness has requested that you attend him.'

Beatrice stared at him in horror. 'You're not serious?' She saw Sayed's face and groaned out loud. 'What does he want to see me for?'

The question almost caused Sayed's leathery face to break into a grin. 'He did not confide in me.'

'And even if he did you wouldn't blab. I know...' She glanced down at the clothes she was wearing. 'I'll have to change.'

Sayed cleared his throat and explained tactfully, 'Actually, I think the request was of the immediate variety.'

'You mean it was a summons?' Beatrice clutched her head and expelled a shaky sigh before firming her mouth. 'Oh well, I suppose I might as well get it over with,' she said, in the tone of a condemned woman. 'I've no idea what he'd want to say to me. Couldn't you just tell him I've booked my flight?'

'Oh, I would imagine he already knows. Little in the palace happens that the King doesn't know about.'

'Did you try and make that sound sinister to spook me out?'

This time Sayed did permit himself a grin.

The King's private apartments were in the oldest part of the palace, and it took a good fifteen minutes before they reached them. Beatrice still hadn't come up with anything he might want to say to her beyond the obvious—Hands off my son—but she had thought of quite a few things she would like to say to him.

The small courtyard she was taken to was a lot less intimidating than the throne room she had imagined. The space was empty but for the King, who sat on a carved stone bench dressed in flowing white robes, his head bare, revealing his leonine silvered mane.

He was reading a book that he set aside when she entered.

'Take a seat, Miss Devlin. You have been with us some time, and we have not had an opportunity to meet before today, but I have been aware of your... actions.'

Did Tariq report to him?

'Tariq has not discussed you with me.'

Tariq, it would seem, had inherited his spooky perception from his father. 'Does everyone have their own set of spies here?' a startled Beatrice blurted.

The King did not look offended. 'I need other eyes and ears, as I do not leave my apartments these days.'

Beatrice decided that on balance she didn't want to know what those eyes and ears had been telling him about her.

'My son...Tariq...he—'

'He—' she cut in, unable to contain the indignation and anger that been building inside her on the way over. 'Tariq—your son—' She broke off, breathing hard as she tried to control her feelings. Her grip of royal protocol was shaky, but even she knew you couldn't tell a king that he ought to consider the consequences his reclusivness had on other people.

'Tariq...?' the King prompted gently.

'I thought you were some sort of invalid—but look at you. You're fine...totally *fine*!'

The King looked startled by the accusation.

'So you need a stick?' she conceded, her glance shifting to the cane at his side. 'And you feel a bit self-conscious about your speech?'

'My people need to see a strong ruler.'

'I'm a stranger, but even I know the people here love you. Have you forgotten that?'

The King's eyes narrowed. His glance was steely as it rested on her face. No slurring was evident as he spoke, a regal warning in his stern voice.

'You forget to whom you speak.'

Of course she had gone too far. But she reasoned it was too late to pull back—and what did she have to lose?

'I know I'm no great loss to diplomacy, and I'm sorry—I know I'm speaking out of turn—but I hate to see Tariq... Oh, I know his shoulders are broad and he's capable—he'd be the first person to tell you he's the most capable person on the planet—' she vented a dry laugh and tucked her hair behind her ears '—and I'm well aware that he's not exactly troubled by lack of self-belief, and I know it will be his job one day. But not yet.'

The King had allowed her to continue speaking partly because her forthrightness had a certain novelty value. But as he listened to what she was saying he wondered if there was not a grain of truth in it. Also, this young woman had the most ex-

pressive face he had ever seen, and he found it entrancing to
watch the expressions flicker across her beautiful face.

'He worries about you, he worries about his brother, and as
dear as Khalid is, I don't see why he gets to swan around playing
the playboy while Tariq does all the hard work. Responsibility
would do him some good. I'm sorry, I know it's none of my
business—and you brought me here to ask me something...?'

She angled a questioning brow and waited tensely for his
response, wondering what the penalty was for telling the King
a few home truths.

'I did. But you have answered all my questions, Miss
Devlin.'

She was worrying about this enigmatic response when he
smiled and asked if she would like some refreshment. As it
clearly wasn't really a request, Beatrice smiled nervously and
took a seat.

CHAPTER TEN

WHEN he had told Beatrice that his father would agree to the marriage Tariq had never doubted his ability to make good his promise.

But he'd been wrong. His father's attitude was totally inflexible. When reasoned argument and persuasion had failed he had resorted to moral blackmail, asking the King if he was willing to sentence his son to a life without the woman he loved at his side.

'He will love again.'

'For some men there is only one love, one soul mate.'

His father had responded to this pressured retort with scornful laughter. There were no circumstances, he had told Tariq, that would make him agree to this marriage between Beatrice Devlin and Khalid.

He'd then said some things about Beatrice that had made Tariq forget the respect his parent was due and resulted in an exchange of harsh words, after which Tariq had stormed out of his father's apartments.

He headed directly for the hospital. His intention was to explain the situation to Khalid and promise his brother he would do everything in his power to change their father's mind, but that it might take some time.

The consultant caught up with him just as he was about to enter Khalid's room. When the medic was finished, he condensed the report.

'So there will be no long-term consequences for Khalid?'

'None,' the doctor agreed cheerfully.

Tariq expressed his gratitude and entered his brother's room. Khalid was sitting in a chair, a phone pressed to his ear as he looked out at the bustling city street far below.

Tariq closed the door quietly and prepared to wait until his brother had finished speaking.

'And I love you, Emma, you know I do, and soon we will— Hey! What—?' He cried out as the phone was snatched unceremoniously from his grasp. 'Tariq! I didn't hear you…'

'But I heard *you*, little brother,' Tariq said as he dropped it in the jug of iced water at the bedside. 'Who,' he asked, in a voice like cold steel, 'is Emma?'

Khalid's eyes fell from his brother's hot, accusing glare. 'I didn't know you were there…'

'Who is she?'

'Oh, all right, then,' he muttered, glaring defiantly at his brother. 'I'm sick of all this pretending anyway. Emma is the girl I love.'

Inside Tariq rage flared hot, but outside he was as cold as ice. 'Yesterday you loved Beatrice.'

'When you meet Emma you'll love her too, Tariq.'

Tariq's jaw clenched. 'I do not transfer my affections quite so easily as you appear to,' Tariq observed sardonically. 'And are you planning on marrying her too? Or are you planning on starting up a harem?'

Khalid flushed at the sarcasm. 'If you must know,' he yelled in a driven voice, 'we're already married. We had a civil ceremony. And Emma is having my baby. And if you and Father don't like it, too bad!'

The colour seeped from Tariq's face. 'Is what you say true?'

'Yes, but—'

'You disgust me!'

Khalid looked shaken by the venom in his brother's voice. 'I didn't want to lie, but Beatrice is—'

Sucking in a breath through flared nostrils, Tariq held up his hand. 'I saw her face when she heard about your accident… She sat by your bed—' He stopped, shook his head, and regarded his brother with contempt. 'If you were not already in a hospital bed I would put you there.'

With a last contemptuous glare at his brother, Tariq walked out of the room.

As she opened the door to allow Tariq to enter, Beatrice was very conscious of her packed cases in the next room.

'I have just been to see Khalid.'

Beatrice looked at his face and her heart sank.

'Something has happened?'

Tariq nodded. 'Yes, it has.'

Beatrice sank into a chair, pale-faced and feeling sick. Emma was even now on her way here, and she had told her Khalid was fine.

'Not that kind of something.'

Her head came up. 'You mean he's all right?'

Tariq's jaw tightened. 'He is well.' That would only be a temporary situation.

Beatrice expelled a long shaky sigh of relief. 'Then what…?'

'There is no easy way to tell you this.' His dark eyes moved over her face before he swung away suddenly, saying something angry in his own tongue.

Beatrice stared at his rigid back, a perplexed frown pleating her brow as he began to pace the room. 'I wish you'd tell me what's wrong, because I promise you I'm imagining all sorts of terrible things.'

'There is another woman.'

Beatrice stared at him. 'Another woman?'

His lip curled in contempt. 'She is called Emily.'

Suddenly comprehension and relief dawned. 'Emma,' Beatrice corrected.

His brows shot up. 'You *know* about her?'

'She's my best friend.'

Tariq swore under his breath. He dropped down and, squatting on his heels so that their faces were level, caught one of Beatrice's hands. 'If he told you he had finished with her I'm afraid he was lying, Beatrice,' he told her gently.

'He didn't tell me that. I know he loves Emma.'

Tariq's brow creased as his dark eyes scanned her face. 'You know he...and yet you are with him?'

His tone made her flush defensively. 'It's not like that,' she protested, wondering why Khalid had only told his brother part of the story.

He shook his head and raised a clenched fist to his forehead as he struggled to control his temper. 'Are you so besotted that you are willing to share him? Have you no pride? No self-respect?' he raged. 'Did you also know that he has *married* this woman?'

Beatrice's eyes widened. 'Married?' she yelped. 'They got married?'

'And she is carrying his child.'

Shock wiped the colour from Beatrice's face. 'A baby!' Beatrice exclaimed, her face registering her amazement at the news.

'You think this is the end of the world,' he said. Beatrice didn't resist as he took her shoulders and pulled her to her feet. 'But it is not,' he promised her. He hooked his thumb under her chin and forced her face up to his. 'You could have any man you wanted.'

The kindness in his voice was her undoing. Tears began to seep from her eyes, streaming unchecked down her face. 'I don't want any man,' she quivered. 'Only one man.'

Anger, molten hot, surged through him as he looked down into her shimmering eyes. His fingers tightened around her upper arms. 'That is not true. You wanted me,' he gritted.

Oh, my God, he knows. With an inarticulate cry of horror she began to pull away, but Tariq jerked her back, causing their bodies to violently collide, knocking the air from her lungs.

The anger rolled off him in waves she could literally feel as he snarled, 'It may not be the pure and elevated emotion you apparently feel for my brother, but you wanted me…you *want* me.'

Standing thigh to thigh, both breathing heavily, they locked eyes.

'I…' As her throat clogged with an emotional thickness Beatrice shook her head.

'Deny it!'

Beatrice lifted her chin, anger lending an extra sparkle to her luminous eyes as she responded to his cruel challenge. 'I can't,' she shouted. 'Are you happy now?'

He didn't look happy. He still looked ferociously angry, the strong angles of his patrician features taut as his burning gaze roamed across the soft contours of her upturned features.

Beatrice felt her anger drain. Her breath quickened and her heart skipped several beats; the stretching silence vibrated with raw sexual awareness.

'I could make you forget him.'

CHAPTER ELEVEN

A FEBRILE shudder slipped down her spine. *You could make me forget my name*, she thought, looking into his sinfully gorgeous face and feeling weak with lust, empty with sheer hopeless longing.

'I know you could.'

The predatory gleam that lit his eyes zapped a thrill of excitement through her body.

'Mabelle...' He lifted his hand to touch her cheek, but Beatrice caught it between her hands and kissed his palm. She heard his sharp intake of breath as she closed her eyes and moved her mouth across the lightly callused surface.

Still holding his hand away from her face, Beatrice lifted her gaze to his. The hunger blazing in his eyes took her breath away. Beatrice struggled to retain control, but it wasn't easy when her entire body throbbed with need. She had to tell him the truth before this went any further.

'Khalid... He's...'

'He is a lying cheat and you still love him... This I already know—but you won't be thinking about him while you are in my bed,' he promised her grimly.

It didn't seem possible to Beatrice that he still thought she was in love with Khalid. She felt as though her feelings were emblazoned in neon across her forehead.

While she didn't want him to guess her feelings, she couldn't allow Tariq to carry on thinking about his brother this way.

'No, Tariq, I—'

He laid a finger to her lips. 'I want to make love to you.'

He leaned closer into her and her vision blurred as Beatrice breathed in the warm male smell of him. It no longer seemed so essential to offer explanations. It just seemed imperative to immerse herself in him.

'I want that too, Tariq.'

He captured her gaze with his eyes, and his own burned as though lit from within, the mesmerising silver lights dancing like flames. 'I will heal you—make you forget.'

You will break my heart, she thought, not actually caring at this point. 'I don't want to forget anything about this, or you.'

This would be a memory she would keep for ever. She knew it would be special, and that Tariq was the man she had been waiting for—even though she hadn't known she was waiting.

His mouth was hot on her, his lips firm as he lowered her to the low sofa, pausing only to sweep the pile of cushions onto the floor first.

His mouth stayed on hers as he unfastened the buttons on her shirt. Beatrice clung and kissed him back, opening her mouth to deepen the sensual penetration of his probing tongue. As he spread the fabric of her shirt she felt the cool air on her hot skin and shivered. The shiver became a feverish tremor when she felt his hands caress the same ultra-sensitive nerve-endings.

Filled with a driving desperation, Beatrice tugged at the waistband of his pants, sliding her hands under the fabric of his shirt to touch his skin.

Her body arched, and she moaned as his lips moved up the white column of her throat. 'I want to feel you against me, your skin on mine,' she whispered in his ear.

Tariq lifted himself off her and fought his way first out of his shirt and then his trousers. Lastly he kicked aside his boxers.

Her fractured gasp as he turned back to her was audible above the thunder of his own heartbeat.

The fact that she was lying there, one hand flung above her head, her breasts visibly rising, staring at him through half-closed eyes, only increased his painful level of arousal.

His hands shook as he began to remove her clothes. Her body

was smooth as silk and soft, and revealing her lush curves filled him with a gloating pleasure. It took all his strength not to sink into her right then.

He was so beautiful, in a raw, primitive and totally perfect way, that it hurt…it physically hurt. Beatrice felt a moment's anxiety. It seemed impossible that a man this perfect, a man who could literally have any woman he wanted, could find anything to admire in her body.

Her soft firm breasts spilled from their confinement as he unclipped the front fastener of her bra. 'You are so beautiful!'

His reverent murmur sent a surge of relief through Beatrice. It was followed closely by delirious delight as he took her breasts in his hands and applied his tongue to first one pink quivering peak and then the other, until she was all need and instinct and no inhibitions.

'Does this feel good? Is this what you want?' he slurred as he lowered himself onto her pale body, one hand braced beside her head and one thigh insinuated snugly between hers, creating just enough pressure and friction to draw a low, keening cry from her throat.

She caught his lower lip between her teeth and tugged softly. Her hands slid cross the hard, glistening, golden contours of his shoulders before she speared her fingertips down his quivering thigh muscles. All the time his eyes held hers captive, and the heat in his bold molten stare made her dizzy.

'Everything you do feels good. That too,' she added huskily, as he slid a hand between her thighs, nudging them gently but firmly apart.

Her eyes closed and a wave of intense heat spread across her skin as he sought her warmth and moisture, touching and stroking her secret inner recesses until she thought she'd die from the sheer pleasure of it. 'I don't think I can talk any more.'

'Talking is not necessary.'

And very soon, much to Tariq's immense relief, neither was restraint. Within a short time Beatrice was writhing under his caresses, begging him for release. He had never known a woman so exquisitely sensitive—just as he had never known this mingling of tenderness and lust with any woman.

The need to claim her, to make her his was like a roar in his overheated blood. It was primal and raw and he could fight it no longer.

She didn't want him to.

A few seconds later he realised she had never been with a man before.

'Relax,' he coaxed, every sinew straining against the iron self-discipline he exerted as he held himself immobile above her, resisting the primitive hunger surging through his body, driving him to sheath himself deep in her tight, slick heat.

'I am,' she moaned. 'Oh...you feel so good. I'm...'

'I don't want to hurt you... Just let me...' As he slid deeper, and she closed around him and with him, he groaned.

Her face pressed into his shoulder, Beatrice said his name over and over, her hands tightening across the sweat-slick skin of his back as he kissed her eyelids.

It was only when he felt the first spasms of her orgasm, when she cried out hoarsely in amazement, that he allowed himself the final thrust deep into her and allowed himself a shuddering release.

Long after the last little orgasmic aftershocks had passed they stayed connected, limbs entwined, warm breaths mingling. In a strange way Beatrice found this sleepy aftermath almost more intimate than the actual sex act they had just shared.

It was only when she felt him stir inside her that she was roused from her sleepy content. Her eyes flickered open, a question in them as she looked up at him.

'I'm not hurting you? You're not sore...?' The streaks of colour across his high cheekbones deepened as he waited for her reply.

'No,' she whispered.

He kissed her. 'This time it will be slow and good for you.'

It was slow, languid, and so exquisitely tender that she wept as Tariq drove her to the brink twice before he responded to her increasingly desperate pleas and carried her over the edge.

'Thank you,' she whispered as she curled up in his arms.

He had given her something precious, something that she would treasure for the rest of her life. She drifted off to sleep, and when she woke the first thing she saw was Tariq's face.

'How is it that your love affair with my brother did not involve actual sex?'

The deceptively mild question effectively wiped the dreamy smile from her face and stilled any unwise declarations of undying love that hovered on her unruly tongue.

A muscle quivered in his lean cheek, but it was his smoothly muscled golden back he presented to her as he queried, in a tone wiped clean of its normal vibrance, 'Well?'

'I was never Khalid's lover or his girlfriend.'

She watched as his eyes closed and he ground the heel of one hand to his head. He swallowed, seeming not to notice the extended silence, before he added in a voice she barely recognized, 'How is this possible…?'

'My friend Emma—she and Khalid…'

Emma. Of course Emma. He sucked in a deep breath. 'You were never Khalid's lover…?' It was still hard for him to take in.

The memory of interminable hours of tortured guilt rose up, and a strangled laugh was dragged from Tariq's throat.

Did irony get any darker than this?

'You made me mad when you tried to bribe me…' She lost her thread as her eyes became fixated on the visible tremor in his long brown fingers as he fastened, or failed to, the buttons on his shirt.

Their eyes meshed briefly, and his dropped first. *Because he can't bear to look at me*, Beatrice thought and wanted to die.

What did you expect, Bea? she asked herself. You've not stopped lying to the man since you laid eyes on him—you've only just stopped lying to yourself! Sure, you came out here because you're a selfless friend… The fact you would have rewritten history if it had meant seeing this man, sharing the air he was breathing again, had nothing to do with it!

'So when Emma and Khalid said you'd never agree to them marrying, I saw a way of having my revenge and solving their problem.'

'This was your idea?'

This time it was Beatrice who couldn't hold his gaze. He hated her, she thought dully.

'I suggested,' she admitted gruffly, 'that he bring me here, and I would be so awful that after me Emma would seem like the perfect wife... Well, actually she is—perfect, that is. Not at all like me.'

A laugh that it almost hurt to hear was wrenched from deep inside him. 'No one is like you, Beatrice.'

Briefly his dark tortured eyes flickered across her face before he rose to his feet.

His back told her nothing as he fought his way into his remaining clothes, none of his normal co-ordination evident in his abrupt, clumsy actions.

'Say something, Tariq,' she pleaded, utterly disconcerted by his behaviour.

'You wanted to make me look foolish. And I obliged.'

She nodded, still confidently expecting an explosion. But none came, and it was disconcerting to put it mildly. His silence made her feel she had to defend her actions.

'You were pretty vile to me, and I didn't know any of *this* would happen!' she told him earnestly. 'I didn't plan this.'

'You did not plan to be seduced,' he said heavily. 'That I can believe.'

'You didn't seduce me,' she protested. 'You made love to me...beautifully,' she added huskily as her eyes dropped from his.

But he had seen her eyes, and her heart was in them, and Tariq longed with every fibre of his being to gather her to him and tell her what was in his heart. He fought the impulse.

He had already done this thing in the wrong order...now he

wanted to make things right. He wanted to come to her free to offer her what she deserved.

'Tariq…?'

'I must… I need…'

For a moment their eyes locked. He added nothing, but her fertile imagination had no problem filling the gap… He needed to put as much space between her and himself as humanly possible!

She would have infinitely preferred it if he had shouted and yelled, but he just continued to stare at her for what seemed like aching hours, then got up and left without another word.

CHAPTER TWELVE

IT WAS the early hours when her flight touched down in London. The ten-hour stop-over had stretched into twelve in Paris, and it was an effort for Beatrice just to put one foot in front of the other. She felt numb with exhaustion. It wasn't the sort of exhaustion that a good night's sleep was going to put right either.

She was so lost in her own dark thoughts that she didn't at first register the person at her elbow. When he invited her for a second time to leave the Customs line and accompany him to his office she was bewildered, but not initially alarmed.

'I think you've got the wrong person. I'm Beatrice Devlin.' She held out her passport to prove the point.

The man barely glanced at it. 'Yes, Miss Devlin, it is you we want.'

'But why?' she protested, aware of the speculative stares of her fellow passengers following her progress.

'Routine. Nothing to worry about.'

Easy for him to say, she thought as she walked past him into what she thought was an office. It turned out to be some sort of plush-looking lounge.

'If you could wait here?'

Before she could ask anything else he was gone.

Beatrice sat down heavily on one of the leather sofas and looked around the bland but pleasant surroundings.

Why do I feel guilty? she asked herself as she struggled to keep her imagination on a leash. She was really annoyed with herself for being so passive and meekly following, no questions asked. When the man came back she would not be so submissive.

There would be a perfectly simple explanation for this. She was, after all, innocent of everything but falling in love with the wrong man. And as far as she knew there was no law against that yet...or half the female population would be locked up.

She got up and walked over to the mirrored panel that lined one wall, grimacing at the sight of her dishevelled appearance. She passed a hand across her pale face and had begun to raise it to smooth her tousled hair when she found herself wondering if this was one of those two-way mirrors she'd seen in films.

She knew the idea was fantastical, but it stuck, and the thought of unseen eyes watching her sent a shudder down her spine.

She laughed and thought, *Pull yourself together—you're losing it.*

'Now, that *is* paranoid, Bea,' she said out loud.

She was about to retake her seat when the door opened. She turned, determined to find out what this was all about.

'Hello, Beatrice.'

The blood drained from Beatrice's face as the world tilted a little—actually, a lot—on its axis. 'You're here...? How...? Why...?'

Tariq, dressed in black jeans and shirt, stood framed in the doorway, looking tall, rampantly male and devastatingly handsome.

'I flew—though rather more directly than you.' His dark stare seemed to pierce her soul. 'As to the why...' His slow smile had an explosive quality that made her heart beat faster.

He covered the space between them in a couple of strides, and before her dazed brain had even coped with the information that he was standing here, now, with her, he took her face between his big hands and covered her mouth with his.

Beatrice's soft cry was lost in his mouth, and she grabbed the front of his shirt and clung to him as he kissed her deeply, as though he would drain the life from her. She kissed him back, responding to the need she sensed in him more than his hunger.

When eventually they broke apart he pressed his nose to hers and took a deep breath. 'Does that answer your question?'

A dazed expression on her face, she lifted her head from his shoulder and looked at his dark, lean features. It seemed doubtful he had flown all this way to kiss her.

'Not really. But it was nice.'

'I think I can do better than *nice*,' he growled, making her stomach flip.

As he moved towards her again she turned her head, even though every cell in her body longed for his lips.

'You shouldn't have come,' she whispered.

He pushed his fingers into her hair and, lifting it from her neck, pressed his lips to the sensitive skin beside her ear, sending a deep shudder of pleasure through her body. 'I had to come. Did you think I would let you go?' he wondered, sounding incredulous.

'You should go. I think they're going to arrest me, and they could be here any moment,' she warned him with a nervous glance towards the door. 'If they find you it could cause a lot of embarrassment.'

'Nobody is going to arrest you,' he said, sounding so tender it brought a lump to her aching throat.

'Well, maybe not, but they…' Her eyes closed as he nuzzled her neck and stroked the angle of her jaw with one finger.

'How do you think I knew you were here, Beatrice?'

Her eyes suddenly blinked wide, and with an accusing cry of, 'It was you!' she spun around. '*You* had them bring me here!' she cried.

'It was a total abuse of power,' he admitted, looking unrepentant. Actually, he looked quite pleased with himself.

'I was terrified! I thought… Everyone was staring at me as though I was a criminal…' Her face scrunched into a pained grimace at the recollection.

'I'm sorry if you were frightened, but I couldn't risk you slipping through my fingers again. Have you any idea what it felt like to find you had run away?' His chin dropped to his chest, but not before she had seen the raw pain in his face.

'I didn't run. I caught a flight.' She struggled to control the deep sob that welled up inside her and failed. She had known he was never going to love her, but to leave thinking that he hated her, that he couldn't stand the sight of her, had been incredibly painful.

But now it seemed he didn't hate her. If only her brain wasn't so whacked with exhaustion she might have been able to make sense of this, but as it was she couldn't seem to string two coherent thoughts together.

His mouth twisted. Her painful dry sob felt like a knife in his chest. 'Please don't cry—the last thing I want to do is make you cry.'

Beatrice pulled out a tissue and blew her nose. 'Well, what do you want? I'm assuming you didn't come all this way just to kiss me?'

His smouldering gaze moved restlessly across her face, pausing on the generous curve of her lips. 'Actually, I was hoping for more than a kiss.'

'You want more than a kiss?' she echoed, angry because he was going to hurt her again, and she was going to let him, because where Tariq was concerned she had no sense of self-preservation.

Where Tariq was concerned she had no sense full-stop!

'I just can't keep up with you!' she raged, giving vent to her frustration. 'First you don't want me to marry Khalid. In fact you'll do anything to stop me. Then suddenly you're moving heaven and earth to try and get us married off. A few hours ago,' she yelled, 'you couldn't get out of my bed fast enough. Now you jump on a plane and follow me halfway around the world to kiss me—sorry, *more* than kiss me. I don't know if I'm meant to be flattered, but I know I'm confused!'

Tariq listened to her impassioned speech and watched the emotions flicker across her tear-stained face, his own expression unreadable. For several seconds after she stopped he didn't move, just stood there, his dark eyes boring into her. Then without a word he reached into the breast pocket of his shirt and pulled out a folded piece of paper, which he opened, smoothed the crease and held out to her.

Beatrice took it warily and glanced down. She found herself looking down at the snapshot taken on the beach in France.

'I have not been acting totally rationally since the moment I looked at that photo.'

Her eyes flew to his face. *Don't let yourself think that*, she cautioned her hopeful heart. *If he ever had any feelings for you he'll never forgive you for tricking him.*

'It's true. Do you know it never occurred to me for one moment to question which woman my brother had fallen in love with? I found no problem believing that my brother would fall in love with you, because I could easily imagine it happening to me.'

The raw emotional intensity in his throbbing voice froze her to the spot.

'I was bewitched by you before we even met, and when we did…'

'You hated me.'

He shook his head. 'I wanted to. For a time I convinced myself that everything I did was to protect Khalid. But the fact was my motives were far less selfless and noble. I was forced to recognise my actions for what they were and I was ashamed. I tried to put things right as a penance—I suppose to assuage my guilt. Thanks to me, Khalid almost lost his life and you the man you loved…or so I thought,' he added heavily.

He extended his hands to her, and after the slightest of hesitations Beatrice took them. She felt the warmth and strength of his fingers as they curled around her own.

'I was jealous.'

Beatrice swallowed, emotion congealed in her throat. The admission from this proud man was something she had never imagined she would hear.

'If I couldn't have you I didn't want anyone else, especially my brother, to have you,' he admitted, with a frown of self-condemnation. 'And to make the situation worse you didn't oblige by being the mercenary, cold-hearted little opportunist I had convinced myself you were. You lost no time showing me how wrong I'd been by rushing around winning hearts, saving children... Yes,' he said seeing her expression, 'Sayed told me about that little adventure.'

'He was your spy?'

'He was my critic once he fell under your spell,' he retorted grimly. 'But even I had to stop pretending that you were not the marvelous, warm and loving woman you are when I saw your reaction to Khalid's accident.'

Her heart lurched. 'I'm marvellous?'

'You, my little love, are totally incredible.'

'What did you just call me?' she whispered.

'You can't be surprised.' His own father knew he was in love with her, so it seemed impossible that she hadn't had an inkling—because according to his parent he had been incredibly obvious.

'Nobody has ever called me little before.'

One dark brow lifted. 'And has anyone ever called you *my love* before?'

'They haven't, and I've never wanted to be anybody's love before,' she admitted almost shyly.

He gave a fierce smile. 'And now?'

Beatrice looked at him with a clear gaze. 'I want to be your love, your lover...'

The hot triumph that flared in his eyes was mingled with relief. 'And my wife?'

Beatrice stared, the blood draining from her face. 'You're proposing to me?'

He looked amazed that she could even ask. 'Obviously.'

'Not to me. You've only known me for a few weeks, and for most of that time you were either hating me or trying to marry me to your brother!'

'We have fitted a lot into a few weeks,' he said drily. 'I once believed that a person could choose when they fell in love, and with whom they fell in love. I know now I was an arrogant idiot.'

'You really want to marry me?' Of course it was out of the question—his father would never countenance such an unsuitable match—but the fact he wanted to was what mattered to Beatrice.

She'd be his lover, his mistress—she'd be whatever he wanted so long as it kept her near him. Right now the details weren't important. The only thing that mattered was the utterly amazing fact that Tariq loved her.

'I've never had a real family. I've never been the most important person in someone's life—' She stopped as her voice became suspended by emotional tears.

Tariq's heart twisted in his chest as he thought of the lonely little girl who had never had a family. The lonely little girl who had grown up and learnt to hide her vulnerability behind a smile and a strong persona. 'You are now, and you have a family.'

Beatrice gave a sad little smile. 'I have you and that's all that matters to me. The marriage thing—well, it's not terribly realistic, is it, Tariq?' He'd probably be relieved that she had realised this. 'If your father wouldn't agree to a marriage between me and Khalid, he's never going to agree to us.'

'I already have my father's permission.'

She blinked like a bemused owl. This was the last response in the world she had anticipated. 'You have?' she exclaimed. 'That's… Oh, no,' she said, starting to shake her head.

'You don't believe me?' Tariq didn't know whether to be angry or amused. 'Where do you think I went when I left you?'

'But you were angry…disgusted with me for tricking you.'

'It is never easy on a man's pride to see he has been made to look a fool, but there were other more important things on my mind at the time. I had made love to you with the intention of wiping out the memory of your other lovers, only to discover there had been *no* other lovers.

'You were an innocent. I was still reeling from the knowledge that I was your first lover, that you had given me something precious. I wanted to make things right. When I went to see my father I was not in the mood for an argument, but I was expecting one,' he admitted. 'His response came as something of a surprise to me.'

Beatrice shook her head. 'He agreed?' she said wonderingly.

'He insisted. He appears to have given the matter some thought already, and he plans to take some of the weight of responsibility from my shoulders so that I can spend some time producing the grandsons he expects us to provide.'

'Babies…' Beatrice, who had not thought that far ahead, lifted her dazed face to Tariq.

Smiling, he watched the rosy flush spread across her face. 'Do you like the idea?'

A smile spread like the sun, illuminating her face. 'I love the idea,' she admitted. 'But I still don't understand. I was actually quite rude to him.'

Tariq looked amused by her confession. 'You must tell me about that one day. But just now I have an urgent and compelling need to hear you say you'll marry me.'

Beatrice reached up and took his face between her hands. 'I love you, Tariq Al Kamal, and I want more than anything to be your wife. But are you totally sure,' she added with a worried frown, 'that this is a good idea? I have a habit of saying the wrong thing, and—'

He placed a finger on her lips to still the flow. 'I want a wife, not a diplomat,' he chided. 'And I have no problem with you speaking your mind. You can say whatever you like, so long as one of the things you say is that you love me.'

'I think I can manage that,' she admitted, looking at him with a love shining in her eyes that spoke louder than any words.

'So that is settled,' he said, sliding his hands down to her bottom and pulling her to him. 'Enough talking. If I don't kiss you right now I will expire.'

'People don't die for lack of kisses,' she teased, running a loving finger down the strong curve of his cheek.

'I wouldn't like to put it to the test,' Tariq admitted as he caught her hand and raised it to his lips. The laughter died from his eyes as he scanned her face and added, 'I could live without you, Beatrice. But it would be only half a life, and I would not be a whole person.'

She was touched too deeply for words by his declaration, and tears of emotion flooded Beatrice's eyes as she raised herself up on tiptoe and pressed her lips tenderly to his.

'You are the best person I know,' she said fiercely. 'I've always taken pride in not needing anyone, but now I'm proud I need you. Take me home, Tariq?'

'To Zarhat?'

'My home,' she said simply, smiling at the discovery, 'is where you are.'

* * * * *

KEPT FOR THE
SHEIKH'S PLEASURE

Lynn Raye Harris

CHAPTER ONE

DR. GENEVA GRAY was asleep in her tent when the ruckus outside awoke her. Last night she'd fallen into bed so exhausted that she'd not undressed. Consequently she had nothing to pull on except her shoes before she stumbled outside in the pre-dawn darkness to see what the commotion was.

A group of riders in traditional desert garb whirled their mounts through the encampment, poking into bags and boxes and upending all the work the team had done in the last several days. Genie cried out as a box broke open and precious artifacts spilled onto the sand.

One of the men on horseback looked up sharply at her cry. A moment later he spurred his horse forward. Genie was riveted to the spot as the horse pounded toward her. It was like a dream, where she was being chased by a huge monster and couldn't seem to move. Her heart thudded, her brain screamed for her to run, but her feet wouldn't work.

Until he was nearly upon her.

Her feet came unglued and she spun to dash behind one of the tents. Behind her, the horse's hooves churned up the sand, coming closer and closer. She managed to duck under a tent flap, then stood and listened carefully for any movement outside. The horse circled the tent. Genie crossed to the other side and waited until she could hear the horse opposite before she made a run for it.

People were screaming and yelling in the night—male voices speaking English, Arabic and Egyptian. If she could just get to one of the Land Rovers she'd be safe. The keys were usually inside—who would steal a Land Rover in the middle of the desert?—and if she could start one up she could use it as a weapon against these intruders. At the very least she could help some of her team to escape.

She could see the cars glinting in the increasing light as she ran.

Almost there, almost there...

Genie had her fingers on the door handle when she was ripped backward and hauled up against a wiry body. Sharp, warm steel rested in the hollow of her throat, and a man spoke in an Arab dialect that it took her a moment to place.

When she did, the pain of bittersweet memories and regret flooded her. She barely had time to remember before everything went black.

She did not know how far they had traveled, or how long she had been unconscious, but when Genie awoke she was surrounded by sound. Soft, lilting sound that grew more excited as she opened her eyes and blinked. A face came into view, hovering over her. And then another.

Women, she realized, with a profound sense of relief.

The women urged her up, then took her to a basin filled with fragrant water. Despite her protests, they undressed and washed her, then refused to let her put her own clothes back on. Instead, they produced a sky blue robe and veil made of silk and tissue and embroidered with gold thread. Genie gave up and pulled the garments on, since hers seemed to have disappeared in the interim. She was thankful, at least in some respects, for the soft material against her skin instead of the coarse cotton of her work clothes.

"Where am I?" she asked, once she'd finished.

But the women could only shake their heads and speak in the dialect she'd earlier recognized as Bah'sharan.

Could she be in Bah'shar? That thought terrified her—and not because she was a prisoner here and had no idea when or how she would escape.

No, it terrified her because of a man. A man whose memory she'd been running from for the past ten years.

The women gave her food and water and left her. By the time they returned at least an hour had passed. They formed a phalanx around her and herded her toward a big goat-hair tent in the center of the cluster. She had no choice but to pass inside. The tent was large, with ornate carpets blanketing the floors and walls. Men in traditional desert garb reclined on the floor, lounging against tufted cushions. A servant moved between them, filling cups from a hammered copper pot.

One of the men began to speak as they walked in. Genie's attention was riveted on him, because he seemed to be talking about her. He was old, with stained teeth and graying hair, and he addressed another man who sat a little higher, and whose place seemed more ornate than the others surrounding him.

Genie followed the old man's hand gestures from her to the other man—

Her heart stopped. Time stood still. The man on the dais gazed at her indifferently, his black eyes and handsome face so cold and hard that she might not have recognized him if she hadn't known him so well.

Used to know him, Genie.

She hadn't seen him since college. She blinked, wondering if her eyes were fooling her—but no, it *was* Zafir.

He was still as exotic and compelling as that last day she'd seen him. The day he'd shattered her heart with the truth. She took a halting step forward. Could she possibly face him again?

She *had* to. Her freedom—maybe even her life—depended on it.

She took another step, but one of the women grabbed her robe from behind and held it fast.

Desperation drove Genie forward. Zafir was her salvation, her hope. He would not harm her—not again. He no longer had the power to hurt her the way he had years ago. For that she would need to love him. And she most definitely did not.

Genie ripped the veil from her head.

* * *

King Zafir bin Rashid al-Khalifa did not care for surprises. He especially didn't care for surprises like this. Many of the desert chieftains still clung to the old ways—he expected that, and he expected to be given gifts they deemed worthy of his station as their king. He'd even expected to be given women, though he did not desire to start a harem. And he'd always known how he would deal with it since to refuse would cause insult.

Later, he might not care whether he caused insult or not. But right now, with his reign so new, he needed these sheikhs to stop feuding and unite behind him. The future of Bah'shar depended upon it.

Yes, he'd expected women. And he'd expected he would take them back to the royal palace and give them jobs in his household. What he had *not* expected was a woman who clearly did not belong here. A woman who made the past crash down on him like an imploding building.

He blinked, but she did not fade away. She stood with her chin thrust up defiantly, her veil clutched in one hand while the other women melted away.

Genie Gray—here in the flesh. The one woman he'd thought understood him.

She hadn't, of course. He'd been taken by her beauty and intelligence, and by the life he'd led for a brief time in an American university. He'd let himself forget that he was a prince of the desert. She had never forgotten.

His gaze slid over her. Her hair, which had always been the color of new copper, was now cropped shockingly short. A memory of him winding it around his fist while he made love to her in his apartment came to him. He shoved it away.

Surprisingly, the short hair suited her—made her seem more feminine rather than less. Heat uncoiled inside him, but he ruthlessly stamped it down. They'd said all they'd needed to say ten years ago.

Sheikh Daud Abu Bakr didn't seem to realize at first that his prize had removed her veil. When he did, however, he began to lumber to his feet.

Zafir stopped him with a word. He wanted them all gone before he confronted this particular *djinn*. "I accept your gift, Sheikh Abu Bakr."

The old man sat back down with a huff. No one said anything else. There was nothing more to say. Zafir waved them all away. They rose and made their bows before filing from the tent.

Genie stood in the same spot she'd occupied since she removed her veil, her gray eyes huge as she watched him.

Zafir leaned back against the cushion. "Well, Genie, what brings you to Bah'shar? I seem to remember you refused my invitation once."

"We were on a dig," she said, ignoring the jibe. "Across the border. Our camp was overrun and I was taken hostage. I have no idea what happened to the others."

"Ah, so it was work. Of course. I should have known."

Work. With her it was always her work. He'd offered her so much more—a life with him as a cherished companion—but she'd refused. He should have known she would do so. He could still remember the look in her eyes when he'd explained why he couldn't ever marry her.

He'd lived in America long enough to know better, but he'd been convinced she loved him. Convinced that she understood—that she would give up everything and come with him.

Her expression hardened. "Yes. Important work. I—"

"Do not worry," Zafir said, cutting her off. "I will find out what happened to your people and make sure everyone is well."

A breath huffed out of her. "Thank you." She twisted the fabric of the veil between her fingers, her eyes dropping away from his for a moment. "And how is your *wife*?"

"I'm sure you mean *wives*," he said coolly. Yes, he'd had to tell her that his father had arranged a marriage when he was a child and that he was expected to honor the agreement. It had nothing to do with love, and everything to do with duty. She hadn't understood.

Duty. It was a word he sometimes wished he'd never heard.

Her head snapped up. "Of course," she said, the tremble of her lips gone in an instant.

He'd wanted to hurt her and he'd succeeded. But now he felt guilty—as if he'd kicked a puppy. "My first wife died," he said evenly. "I am divorced from the second."

Genie blinked. "Oh. I'm sorry," she added.

Zafir shrugged. It was what people always said, and yet he could not accept it without feeling the usual well of loneliness—and guilt—within. He'd been alone most of his life; being married had not changed that. In some ways it had actually made it worse.

Jasmin had died because of him. And Layla? Layla had surely done what she had because of him as well.

Death, it seemed, followed him.

"These things happen," he said, because he had to say something. "And my second wife would have made a terrible queen, so divorce was not such a bad choice in that case."

Though he certainly hadn't divorced Layla for her inability to be a queen.

Genie's eyes widened. "Qu-queen? But you weren't…"

"The Crown Prince?" he finished. "No, I was not."

Once again death had played its part in forcing his life along paths he would not have chosen.

"My brother has been gone for a year now. My father died a month ago. I am now King of Bah'shar."

She looked stunned. Yes, he could well imagine. It was not what he'd ever expected to do. Not what he'd wanted or studied so hard for. He'd gone for an engineering and architecture degree so he could build things while his older brother prepared to be king. Together they would take Bah'shar into the future, make her bigger, better, more capable than she had been under the rule of their father.

Now he had to do it alone. Always, always alone.

Genie dipped her chin to her chest and swallowed. When she looked up again, her eyes were clear. "I'm sorry for your loss, Zafir. For both your father and your brother."

"Thank you."

"I've taken enough of your time," she continued. "If you could return me to my camp now, I'd be grateful."

Resentment flared to life inside him. She'd been the only woman—the only person, really—he'd ever felt close to. The only one who'd ever seemed to stem the tide of loneliness within him. But to her it had meant nothing. Like every other woman he'd ever known, she'd been with him because of what he was, not who he was inside.

She'd seemed different from the others, but the reality was that he'd been too taken with her to see the truth. She was no different than Jasmin or Layla or any of the women he'd ever dated.

He stewed with hate, regret, and, yes, even desire—and she stood there, completely unaffected. He had a sudden urge to punish her, to show her what she'd given up and could never have again. "How grateful?"

She blinked. "I'm sorry?"

He climbed to his feet. She took a step back as he moved toward her. He refused to let it bother him. Once she would have rushed into his arms. Once she would have melted beneath him.

He stopped in front of her. Her head tilted back, her gray eyes searching his. For a moment he could almost think he was somewhere else. Another time, another place.

Zafir couldn't stop himself from touching her hair. The contact was brief, but her mouth opened, her tongue darting out to moisten her lips. Need rocketed through him. Need he forced away.

"And how well do your pickaxes and pottery shards keep you warm at night, *habiba*? Is it all you thought it would be?"

She glared at him. "You know that's not the only reason why it didn't work out between us. You lied to me, Zafir."

He almost laughed. No one dared to talk to him the way she did—certainly not now that he was king. "I told you the truth, *habiba*."

"You should have told me from the beginning."

"We did not know each other well enough."

She looked outraged. "You were engaged, Zafir, and you slept with me for six months without ever letting me know that fact. I don't think knowing each other had anything to do with it! You didn't want anything to interfere with your ability to get me into bed."

He couldn't stop the smirk that crossed his face. "As if that was so difficult, Genie."

She blushed, and he knew she was remembering their first night together. Their first date. She hadn't been a virgin, but she hadn't been experienced either.

"I'd like to go back to my camp now," she said primly.

"Of course you would," he said, coming to a decision. "And yet I am afraid this is not possible."

Her head snapped up, her eyes blazing suddenly. "What do you mean, not possible?"

He almost had fun saying the next part. Almost, but not quite.

"Because I have need of you here."

CHAPTER TWO

GENIE'S heart dropped to her toes. Next came rising irritation. He was toying with her, punishing her for what happened between them ten years ago. The sex between them had been great, yes, but hers was the only heart that had been affected. She'd been in love with him, and all he'd wanted was to take her to Bah'shar and keep her as a plaything while he married someone else.

Even had he not been engaged she'd been right to break it off between them. He would have prevented her from making something of herself, from pursuing the career she'd always wanted. He would have stifled her freedom and bound her up in a perfumed prison.

She was *glad* she'd refused to go with him. He hadn't loved her and would have discarded her as soon as he'd tired of her. It'd been the hardest thing she'd ever done, walking away from him, but it had been right.

And now he was a king, and trying to use that power to prevent her from returning to her job, her life. Fury whipped through her.

"This is beneath you, Zafir," she said, as coldly as possible.

One dark eyebrow arched. My God, how could the man still be so absolutely breathtaking—especially when he was being so arrogant? And how could she want him as much as she ever had?

"Beneath me? Interesting choice of words, *habiba*."

She folded her arms over her chest. There wasn't much she could control here, but she had to insist on that which she could. "I wish you wouldn't call me that."

He laughed. "Does it bring up bad memories?"

"No," she said automatically. And then, realizing what she'd admitted, followed it with an emphatic, *"Yes."*

"Interesting. I do not remember you objecting when you screamed my name in pleasure, or afterward when I held you close and called you *habiba*."

A sliver of desire sizzled to life inside her. She'd been with a few men in the last ten years, but none had ever affected her the way Zafir had. The way he was affecting her now.

But she'd never seen him like this either. Surely that was what had her blood pumping into her veins like a runaway train? Though she'd known he was a desert prince, he'd never dressed in the tradition of his home when they were together.

He was truly magnificent in the white *dishdasha*. A gold *igal* held his headdress in place, and at his waist was a curved ceremonial dagger with a jeweled hilt.

He was exotic and forbidden in a way he never had been when he'd worn jeans and button-down shirts. When he'd simply been handsome and sexy and she hadn't been able to believe he was hers. That *she* was the one he spent time with when there were so many gorgeous women he could have chosen instead.

Except he hadn't really been hers, had he?

"That's in the past," she forced out. A past that had never really stopped haunting her.

He turned away in a swirl of robes. "I did not say, by the way, that I would *never* let you return to your dig."

Genie shook her head. "I don't understand, Zafir. What do you want from me?"

"The short answer is that my father had trouble with warring tribes in this region. I am here because I intend to put a stop to it once and for all. Since you were a gift from the chieftain of one of the tribes, I can hardly let you leave."

Genie's jaw went slack. "A gift? Like a goat or a camel or a jeweled dagger?"

"Precisely. And until I conclude this meeting I require your presence."

For the moment, she could only focus on the fact that she'd been *given* to him. "How can someone give away a human being? What kind of king are you to allow such a thing to happen?"

His jaw was firm. "I am the king of a very old and traditional nation. The ways of the desert are ancient and cannot be changed overnight."

"But you could have refused."

He crossed his arms, one eyebrow arching. "Indeed I could have. And you would now likely be back in Sheikh Abu Bakr's harem, awaiting *his* attentions."

She thought of the old man who'd been speaking earlier and shivered. "That's barbaric."

"It is the custom."

"You have a lot of customs, don't you?" she said bitterly. Like keeping mistresses while marrying another woman and having children with her.

"Indeed—which is why you will remain."

"And what if I don't want to stay?"

His dark eyes glittered. "You do not have a choice."

"You would force me to stay here against my will?"

He inclined his head. "To prove I am not such a barbarian, I will compensate you in the end. This is not a bad deal, Genie."

For who? Staying here for even a minute longer than she had to was dangerous. Because in spite of everything—all the hurt and pain and agony of the past—her heart was soaring with every minute she stood near him.

"I don't want money."

He looked skeptical. "Really? Aren't archaeological digs expensive?"

"I have funding for my projects." Not as much as she'd like, but she wasn't admitting that to him.

"Then I will give you something better than money, Genie. Something you want very much."

Genie's knees felt suddenly weak. She had a vision of him naked, of his beautiful mouth on her flesh, taking her to heaven *No.* "How could you possibly know what I want?"

His smile was so self-assured she itched to slap him.

"I will give you permission to excavate in Al-Shahar."

Her heart nearly stopped. "The old temples?"

No one had *ever* been given permission to excavate the Temples of Al-Shahar. It would be a coup, a crowning achievement. Her career would never be the same.

And he knew it. His smile was predatory, as if he knew she would not refuse. Just as he'd believed she wouldn't refuse his proposition ten years ago because he'd been rich and handsome and she'd loved him desperately.

Did she have the strength to turn him down this time? The strength to walk away from the Temples of Al-Shahar? But how could she accept? Staying with him now, even for something so wonderful as those temples, would test her in ways she wasn't sure she was prepared to endure.

But he would keep her here regardless, wouldn't he? He had the power to do it, and the will.

"I would not refuse this, were I you," he said softly. "Don't be a fool because of your wounded pride, Genie."

She stiffened. "You are quite mistaken if you still think that affects me, Zafir. It was ten years ago."

"Then what will it be?" Again that predatory gleam. "Because turning down the jewel in the crown of your precious career would be extremely foolish. And you know it quite well."

She hated that he had her right where he wanted her. Because he was right, and she wasn't going to refuse. No matter how dangerous staying with him would be to her heart, she had to do it. It was only temporary. It would take weeks to gather what she needed to excavate in Al-Shahar, so she would have time to recover from this experience. And she need not see him when she returned. He was a king now, and she was an archaeologist who would be on a dig in his city. She had a team who would coordinate with whomever in his government handled these things.

They would not meet again. And, even if none of that were the case, she couldn't let him see that, contrary to what she said, she was still very much affected by the past.

"Very well," she said, holding out her hand. "I accept."

Zafir took her hand in his. Instead of giving a firm shake, he turned her palm up and brought it to his lips. A shiver trickled across her nerve-endings on tiny feet, bringing goosebumps to the surface.

"A wise decision," he said softly.

And then he tugged her into his arms and kissed her.

In the space of a few moments he'd decided he was going to have her again. This need buffeting him was stronger than he remembered. He'd always been enchanted with her body, but had he always felt this reckless desire to possess her no matter the cost?

Surely not. Because right now he wanted to rip the turquoise *abaya* from her body and lower her onto the furs in his tent. He wanted to lose himself in her, and he wanted to remember what it had been like between them.

The heat, the passion, the pleasure.

She'd filled that hole inside him that no one ever had, and yet he couldn't call it love. He hadn't been in love with her. But he'd needed her.

He didn't need her anymore, but he wanted her.

Her mouth parted, whether in surprise or compliance he did not know. But he took advantage of the situation, slipped his tongue against hers—and was rewarded with a sharp intake of breath. Her arms went around him, her body pressing to his so sweetly. If not for the dagger she would be able to feel the effect she still had on him.

He held her close, slanted his mouth over hers to take as much as she would give.

And she gave far more than he would have believed. Proud, beautiful Genie kissed him like a woman starved. Like a woman who'd suffered drought and deprivation and had finally stumbled into an oasis of plenty.

She still wanted him, and the knowledge fired something primal in his blood.

Zafir cupped one of her breasts beneath the soft fabric, groaned low in his throat. He wanted to bare her body and feast his eyes and senses upon her. But he could not do so here—not in the reception tent. He swept her up into his arms and strode toward his sleeping quarters.

Genie clung to him, still kissing him, her passion as hot and intense as ever. He didn't break the kiss, though he had to keep his eyes open to see where he was going. Her skin was flushed a pretty pink, and her long auburn lashes fanned across her cheeks. He wanted her to open her eyes, to look at him with those deep pools of rainwater-gray, to see the passion flaring in them as he made love to her.

A guard stood at attention as Zafir passed into the interior of his private quarters. He set Genie on her feet. She seemed suddenly wild-eyed as her gaze darted around the room—as if she'd awakened in a prison cell instead of a palace.

"Patience, little one," he murmured as he unhooked the ceremonial dagger and tossed it aside.

But when he took her in his arms again she stiffened, her hands coming up to brace against his chest. "No, Zafir," she gasped. "I can't."

Frustration and disappointment spiraled through him at once.

"Ah, so this is how it will be. I should have known." He loosened his hold and she jerked away, wrapping her arms around herself as if she were chilled.

"What's that mean?" she snapped.

"You know what it means, Genie. You tell me one thing with your body and another with your mouth."

Her chin tilted up, her eyes flashing. "I agreed to stay for the chance to excavate in Al-Shahar. I did not agree to sleep with you ever again."

His body pounded with the need for release, and she looked

at him as if she'd *not* just been wrapped around him, wanting him as much as he wanted her.

She was very much the ice-cold scientist she'd always wanted to be. And that infuriated him. How dared she think *she* was the one in control here?

"Perhaps I wish to attach new conditions to the agreement."

Her eyes widened. "You wouldn't."

He took a step toward her, fury whipping him. "Do not presume that you know me any longer, *habiba*. The man I was back then is dead."

"You would blackmail me into your bed simply to get back at me? To punish me because I didn't want to be your plaything for however long you wanted me?"

Her words stung his conscience. And yet…he didn't care. He was angrier than he'd been in a very long time. Angry with fate, with her, and with the stubborn sheikhs who argued over territory and made his life difficult when all he wanted was the best for his people.

He focused on the woman before him. She tried hard to hide it, but she was flushed, her lips moist and plump from kissing, her nipples jutting through the soft fabric of the *abaya*. Not the ice-cold scientist after all.

He was tired of games, tired of lies.

"It is hardly a punishment, *habiba*. Not when we both know what we want."

CHAPTER THREE

GENIE couldn't stop the tremor that slid along her spine. But was it the excitement of what he offered her with the temples, or the thrill of knowing that with one word she would share his bed again?

No. She would not do so. Could not.

"Not everything we want is good for us," she said. "Bacon double cheeseburgers with chili-cheese fries, for instance. All that fat and cholesterol." She was babbling, for God's sake, but she couldn't seem to help it.

Zafir merely shot her that sexy grin that had always been her undoing. "Do you or do you not want the exclusive right to excavate the temples?" he said silkily. "No other archaeologist has ever been allowed to do so."

Genie swallowed. With one kiss he'd stolen her breath, her sense, her will. She'd turned into a needy animal, wanting—no, *craving*—what he offered. If he'd pushed her down on the carpets there and then and lifted her abaya, she'd have been helpless to refuse.

It was only when he'd stopped kissing her, when she'd re-alized they were in what must be his private tent, that she'd asked herself what the blazes she was doing. She'd been about to negate ten years of her life with that single act. To propel herself back in time and into the arms of the man she'd never really stopped loving.

Never depend on a man, Genie. Make your own career, your own life, and find a partner to share it with. But don't give up your goals for him. Because he might just leave you with nothing but broken dreams in the end.

Genie shivered. Her mother had said those words to her so often that she could repeat them in her sleep. Zafir was exactly the kind of man her mother had warned her about.

She'd loved him, but he hadn't loved her. She'd realized it that night when he'd asked her to come to Bah'shar. She'd thought he was asking her to marry him, but she'd been confused because he hadn't said the words. He'd never said he loved her, had always pushed aside questions of his feelings with more kisses and more lovemaking. And just when she'd thought he'd asked her to share his life, her dreams had been crushed into dust by the realization that he was expected to marry another.

It had been cruel, too ironic, that she should find herself in the situation of loving a man who could never marry her.

She'd known his culture was different, that what he asked was not wrong or immoral to him and his world, but there had been no way on earth she could subject herself to the humiliation. She'd seen firsthand what loving a man who would never be yours did to a woman.

To her mother.

And she was not about to endanger her heart and her hard-earned independence by falling into bed with Zafir bin Rashid al-Khalifa ever again.

"I want the commission, Zafir. But not at the price you're asking."

"And what price is that, Genie? I am asking you to share my bed—something you've done many times before." He paused, let his gaze slide down her body. "Or have I erred? Do you have a lover? Someone to whom you wish to be faithful?"

She dropped her eyes from his and shook her head. She should lie, but she found she could not. "There is no one right now."

"Then there can be no problem, can there?"

What could she say? *Yes, there is a problem! The problem is that I still care for you and I'm afraid what will happen if I succumb to my desire instead of listening to my head!*

"The answer is still no, Zafir."

His gaze was laser-sharp. "You would really give up this commission for something so simple?"

"It's not simple in the least, and you know it."

"Why is that, I wonder?" He closed the distance between them, tilted her chin up with a finger. "It is simply sex between two adults who want each other. How can there be a problem with that?"

"I've traveled this road with you before, Zafir. I'm not prepared to do it again."

"And I thought you would sell your soul to the devil himself for the sake of your career."

"That's not fair and you know it. It wasn't my career that ruined it between us." Her breath caught at the silky stroking of his fingers along her jaw.

Apprehension whispered over her like a caress as he smiled. "No, but you *will* share my bed again. Willingly, eagerly, and without hesitation. I guarantee it."

Genie awoke in the middle of the night, shivering. For a moment she didn't know where she was. But then it all came crashing back.

The desert. Zafir. Shock. Desire. Anger. Hurt.

Loneliness.

She sat up, her eyes adjusting to the dim light from the brazier in the middle of the tent. She lay on a large feather mattress, piled high with furs, but she'd somehow managed to kick them all away in the night.

Reaching for a fur, she realized there was a large shape in the bed with her. A man.

Zafir.

He'd left her here last night, telling her to get some sleep. She'd thought she might be shown to her own tent, but he'd informed her there was no other place to go—unless she wanted to go to Sheikh Abu Bakr's harem.

She definitely did not.

So she'd climbed into this bed and fallen asleep, never

realizing he'd returned. And she could clearly see what the problem was now that he was here. Zafir had always stolen the covers.

She tugged the fur away, putting as much distance between them as possible.

"What is wrong, Genie?" he asked, his voice gravelly with sleep.

"You took the covers."

"Never."

She could almost laugh if this situation weren't so surreal. Because he'd always denied stealing the covers when she'd awakened in the night in his apartment.

"It's a bad habit of yours, and you know it."

His laugh sent heat spiraling through her. "So you have always said. My wife said the same, so perhaps it is true."

Now, *why* was her heart throbbing at the thought of another woman knowing him so intimately? It wasn't a surprise, after all. A wife *would* notice those things. She didn't bother asking *which* wife.

He propped himself on an elbow. There was the gulf of the bed between them, but still it felt too intimate to be here like this. Too right and too wrong at the same time.

"Has there been anyone special in your life?" he asked, almost as if he could see the wheels turning in her head as she thought about him with a wife.

"Yes," she said automatically, because she couldn't bear to tell him the truth. That *he* had been the only special man in her life.

"Then I am sorry it didn't work out."

"Me too." Now, why did that bring a well of tears to her eyes? And why did she have to work so hard to keep them from falling?

"Much has happened in the last ten years, has it not? Have you been as successful as you'd hoped?"

"I've done well enough," she said. But what was success, really, when she spent her days poring over old documents and maps, living in harsh conditions while she dug pottery shards from ancient dirt? It was what she'd wanted, what she'd worked for, and yet there was something empty about it too.

She'd thought, after Zafir, she might meet a man who shared her love of ancient history—a fellow archaeologist who wanted all the same things she wanted.

And yet though she'd met plenty of men who might fit those criteria, none of them had touched her heart the way Zafir had.

"You will be pleased to know, by the way, that everyone on your team is accounted for. The men who attacked your camp have been disciplined. Unfortunately you were caught between those warring factions I told you of earlier."

Her guilt at nearly forgetting about her colleagues when her senses were so overwhelmed with Zafir was somewhat allayed by the news that they were all well.

"I should be there to help them collect everything. It will need to be catalogued again, and—"

"They are aware that you are a guest of the King of Bah'shar."

The King of Bah'shar. It gave her a chill to think of Zafir as king, and yet it seemed appropriate too. He'd always been larger than life—and he'd been the only person she'd ever known who had a security detail in college. She'd never been able to forget he was someone important. Imagining a life with him had been impossible. How true that had turned out to be.

"And how much longer am I to remain your *guest*?" In her earlier excitement about the temples she'd forgotten to ask how long he intended to keep her here. *Stupid, Genie.*

"A few days, no more."

"What am I supposed to do for a few days? Stay in this tent? Isn't there another way?"

"We will not be staying. Tomorrow we return to Al-Shahar."

"But I thought you had to stay here…"

"I am the King, *habiba*. I go where I wish. Tomorrow I wish to return to Al-Shahar. My meeting with the Sheikhs will continue there."

"Why can't you just tell them to do what you want? You *are* the King, after all."

His sigh was audible. "Yes, one would think it *should* work that way. But Bah'shar is an ancient country, and things have always been done a certain way. Blood feuds often go back many generations. My father tended to ignore the violence so long as the Sheikhs paid their obeisance."

"Why can't you do the same?" Not that she thought violence should be ignored, but she wanted to know why it was important to him.

"I could, I suppose. But then things happen—like border raids, where old fools let their men kidnap Western archaeologists. It makes us look bad in the eyes of the world. I wish us to move forward as a people, not wallow in the past."

"Isn't tradition important?"

"Of course. But so is progress. And I believe we can have both—though there are those who resist."

"I remember that you were going to build skyscrapers. Do you ever get to do that?"

He sighed again. "I did, for a while. Perhaps once I've settled into this new role as king I will be able to do so again."

They'd only been together six months, but she remembered his enthusiasm for building—his sketches and grand plans. He'd been in love with the idea of creating and she'd been in love with him. God.

"I'm sorry things didn't work out the way you'd hoped," she said.

"It is as it was intended to be. I accept that." He threw back the covers and sat up. "Are you tired?"

"Not really." Too much adrenaline in one day. And too much shock.

"Then come. I wish to show you something." He hesitated a moment. "You once told me you could ride. Was that the truth?"

"Yes, but I won't be joining the Olympic equestrian team anytime soon."

His teeth flashed white in the dim light as he stood and held out his hand. "That is sufficient."

Genie stared at his outstretched fingers. Did she really want to go anywhere with him? To risk even a moment more in his company than absolutely necessary?

But what was the alternative? Refuse and have him climb back into the bed with her?

She put her hand in his. Electricity snapped along her nerve endings, sizzling into her core.

No matter how she sliced it, she was in big trouble here. A few days might as well be an eternity.

"What do you think?" Zafir asked.

Genie could only stare at the undulating sand dunes—no *mountains*—spreading as far as the eye could see. She'd excavated in the desert before, she knew what sand dunes looked like, but she'd never seen anything so beautiful as the pink tinged dawn sky, the red sand that glistened with moisture which would soon be burned off by the hot rays of the sun—and she'd certainly never witnessed it from the back of a white Arabian mare.

The horse's delicately arched neck belied her strength. She'd run up this mountain of sand as fleet-footed as a gazelle. Now she stood, her nostrils flaring, her proud head held high, her bridle dripping with tassels that shook with each prancing movement.

Genie turned in the saddle. Zafir was staring at her. He sat his mount so easily, the white fabric of his *dishdasha* a sharp contrast with his stallion's bay flanks. He looked at home here, regal and otherworldly—like someone she should never have met in a million years.

"Well?" he prompted.

"It's amazing, Zafir."

He turned his head, his profile to her as he gazed over the dunes. It stunned her to realize that he very much looked like a king. How had she never noticed that royal bearing of his?

"I wanted to show you this before, but it was not possible. I am glad you are here to see it now, despite the circumstances."

Her heart throbbed. Why did he have to do this to her? Why did he have to remind her of how much she'd once loved him?

"I'm glad too," she said, though she wasn't really sure if that was the truth. Far better to be over the border, still in her encampment, digging through sand and rock and not knowing Zafir was here—so close and yet so far. In many ways, though he sat beside her now, he was farther from her than he'd ever been.

Untouchable. Unapproachable. A king.

Genie sucked in a cool breath. The desert air was frigid at night, but it was beginning to warm as the sun crept upward in the sky. Soon it would be too hot ever to believe it had been cold only hours before.

Zafir threw one leg over his horse's head and jumped to the ground. "Let us walk before we return to the camp," he said.

Genie dismounted and fell in beside him. They walked along the top of the dune without speaking. The sand made it difficult to go fast, so they took their time—almost as if it were a companionable morning stroll.

Like they'd used to do when they'd get up early and make the walk to the bakery first thing in the morning. "Should we get the donuts or the sunflower bread?" she said, and then wished she hadn't. How ridiculous to bring that up!

But he glanced over at her and smiled. "The donuts, of course."

"That was a simpler time," she said softly, not looking at him. Simpler because she hadn't known what was expected of him, because she'd believed they shared something deep and meaningful. How wrong she'd been.

"Indeed. But everyone grows up, Genie. Life does not sit still because we wish it to."

"No."

He stopped and turned toward her. His face was limned in

the dawn light, the hard planes and angles both harsher and more beautiful because of it. Dark eyes gazed at her intently.

"There is no reason why we can't recapture some of that feeling," he said.

Her heart thudded in her throat, her temples. A few hours ago she'd been Dr. Geneva Gray, renowned archaeologist. Now she was Genie Gray, the lovesick student who'd once had a passionate affair with a desert prince.

And he was tempting her with the promise of more. How could she want him again when he'd hurt her so deeply?

"I'm not sure that's wise," she said.

But he closed the distance between them, his body so close, so vibrant in the cool morning air. "Why wouldn't it be, Genie? We are adults, and we still want each other. This is not a crime."

"No, but it feels too much like digging up the past."

His smile was almost mocking. "Ah, but isn't this what you like to do? Dig up the past?"

"Not all things need to be dug up," she replied, her pulse hammering in spite of how calm she tried to sound.

His head dipped toward her in slow motion. She knew she should move away, but she closed her eyes automatically, waited for the touch of his lips against hers.

It didn't happen.

She opened her eyes again, to find he'd stopped only inches from her mouth.

"I do not believe what you say, Genie Gray. And neither, it seems, do you." He straightened and turned toward his mount. "Come, we must return to the camp before the sun is up."

CHAPTER FOUR

GENIE had never been to Al-Shahar before. Though the city was ancient, and rife with ruins to be explored, Zafir's father had not allowed any excavation to take place. Nor had the previous kings before him. Zafir was the first to suggest it was possible, and she had to admit that the prospect excited her. She had to hope that he would still allow her to do so, regardless that he'd claimed she first had to sleep with him in order to get the commission.

He'd not mentioned it since last night, and she wondered if perhaps he'd merely been angry and acting on emotion from the past instead of truly intending to force her into his bed.

Not that it would take much to force her, she thought disgustedly. In spite of everything—the hurt and pain and anger—she still felt something in his presence. Something she'd never felt with anyone else. Was she adult enough to handle a casual affair? To know he was a king and that he could never, ever have a real relationship with her beyond the physical?

She turned her attention to the city as they passed through the ancient gates at one end. The ruins of the old temples sat on a point that was higher than the rest of the city, with the exception of the palace. She could see them clearly in the distance as she sat up straighter and pressed her face to the glass.

"You want very much to get your hands into the dirt there, don't you?"

She turned to the man sitting beside her. He was still dressed in the robes of the desert, but the ceremonial dagger was gone.

And he was still as breathtaking as he had been from the firs
moment she'd seen him again.

"You know I do. It's a fabulous opportunity, Zafir."

She expected him to tell her that she knew what she had to
do to gain the commission, but he said nothing of the sort.

"I would not have offered it to just anyone—no matter tha
it's past time this city's history was explored and preserved fo
future generations."

Warmth blossomed. "I appreciate your confidence in me."

He shrugged and turned away. "You must be very good a
what you do."

"Must be?" she asked. "Shouldn't you find out before yo
hand over this commission to me?"

His gaze was sharp, assessing. "Should I give you this com
mission, there will be no need."

"I'm not sure how you can say that. It's important work, an
you should get the best to do it."

And why was she saying this? Why place any doubt in hi
mind?

Because she wanted him to *know* she was the best, not just t
give it to her because she was the only archaeologist he knew
Assuming he did so, of course.

Zafir gave her a hard look. "Your work is the most impor
tant thing in the world to you. More important than anyon
or anything. No one would sacrifice so much without bein;
determined to succeed."

A pang of hurt throbbed to life inside her. "It's not the mos
important thing. There's my mother, my friends—"

"But not a lover, yes?"

"I don't need a lover to prove I care about things other tha
work."

He merely shrugged again. "As you say, then."

"*Are* you going to give me the job?"

"That depends on you, Genie."

Genie tamped down on the irritation uncoiling within her. Sh
wasn't about to ask him what he meant. She didn't need to.

She turned to watch the city glide by. Al-Shahar was mor

modern than she'd thought it would be. Cars rolled down wide streets with tall glass and steel buildings. There were sidewalks, manicured trees and plants, and designer shops lining the streets on both sides. It was still early enough that people populated the sidewalks—the men in business suits or traditional robes, the women either wearing colorful *abayas* or Western clothes.

They also passed through an older section of town, where the buildings were mud-brick and she saw more than one donkey pulling a laden cart. The air smelled of spice, exotic and fresh, and she wished she could get out and explore the old bazaars. But the Hummer continued toward the palace, finally passing through the arched gates and pulling to a halt in front of huge double doors that looked as if they were made of gold.

Zafir's door popped open. Someone had unrolled a red carpet, and he stepped out onto it, then turned and held out a hand for her. She accepted, scooting across the seat and joining him on the walkway. The car door slammed again and the vehicle moved away—everything a perfectly coordinated dance of efficiency.

Black-clad men with headsets and Uzis flanked the palace doors, while several other men fanned out behind them.

"Is it so dangerous here you need this many guards?" she asked.

Zafir frowned. "Not at all. It is simply custom."

Another thought wormed its way into her consciousness. A worrying thought. "Zafir, you said you were putting an end to an old feud in the desert. Are you in any danger from those men?"

The double doors whisked open and they passed inside while men and women bowed low. It was disconcerting to be reminded so forcefully at every turn how exalted a being Zafir now was.

And he'd wanted to renew their physical relationship? With a woman who crawled around in dirt and mud on a regular basis? She was beginning to doubt his sincerity on that score.

He stopped at another ornate door. "I am not in danger, *habiba*. Do not worry yourself."

"I wasn't worried," she lied. And she didn't believe him. He'd said there were those who clung to the old ways and didn't want change. When people felt threatened, they were capable of many things. In a volatile environment such as this, would someone go so far as to try and harm the King?

"Go with Yusuf," Zafir said. "He will show you to your quarters. I will see you for dinner tonight."

She could only stare after him as he turned to go.

But then he looked back at her. "And be sure to wear something sexy, Genie."

Zafir entered his private office and went to his desk to see what papers his secretary had left for him. But his mind was on the woman he'd left standing in the hall. It was dangerous to want Genie Gray again. He had too many things he needed to do as a new king trying to cement his rule. Distractions were unwelcome.

Most of his father's ministers had accepted him as king, though there were those who grumbled he'd spent too much time in the West, that his education in America was dangerous to tradition and custom. He was careful to pick his battles, and swift to act once he had. This issue with the blood feuds was one he intended to put a stop to as quickly as possible.

Now that he was king, he was also being pressured to marry again. A king needed heirs, and his ministers were anxious he should get started on the task. He would do so in his own time, however.

His experience with marriage thus far had not been the most pleasant. Jasmin's death had shocked him. She'd been impulsive and high-strung, and when she'd threatened to do herself harm he'd not believed her.

He still didn't believe she'd meant to kill herself.

She'd most likely meant to scare him when she'd taken the pills. She'd counted on him to find her, to call an ambulance, but he'd been delayed that day. By the time he'd found her—it had been too late. He still blamed himself for not taking her seriously, for not getting her the help she needed.

Four years after her death he'd bowed to the pressure to marry again. A mistake.

And now Genie was here, back in his life by accident when he'd never expected to see her again. Her presence brought a feeling of normalcy to the circus his life had become. She'd known him before, when he had been simply Prince Zafir, when he'd been excited about his studies and the things he would build.

Perhaps it was wrong to keep her here, but he didn't care. Because she gave him something he'd thought lost, something he hadn't realized he needed until she'd ripped off her veil in the tent.

Genie Gray gave him a sense of himself as he'd used to be. She made him feel less alone in this world, and he truly needed that right now. Oddly enough, he also felt a pang of guilt over the way they'd parted ten years ago. Perhaps he should have told her about his arranged marriage when they'd first met. Perhaps he should have given her the chance to decide for herself if she wanted to take the risk of being with a man who came from a world so different from her own.

And what choice are you giving her now?

He shoved the thought aside brutally. He would not force her into his bed, no matter what he'd told her. He'd been angry, and he'd said things he did not mean.

But he *would* bed her again. It was as inevitable as the sandstorms that swept across the desert.

Genie stood in the middle of the cavernous quarters she'd been shown to—the old harem, Yusuf had explained—and studied the tilework over her head. The room was vaulted, the mosaic inlaid with gold and precious gems. It was an extraordinary room.

There were marble columns, soaring arches, stained glass, and a crystal chandelier that must stand twice as tall as she if it were lowered to the floor and she could measure herself against it.

This room connected to another—a smaller room this time,

with a large bed on a dais in the center. The furnishings were ornate, more modern than appropriately suited this space, and luxurious. She went through another door and found a bathroom that would more or less be considered a spa where she lived. A cutout high in the roof let natural light in, and it shafted down over a pool—yes, *pool*—from which steam arose.

A natural hot spring. Marvelous.

On a long shelf there were scented oils and cosmetics in an array of delicate blown-glass bottles. She passed into another room, and came up short. This was a dressing room, and one wall was lined with clothes. But whose clothes? His ex-wife's? A mistress's?

She plucked at the first garment. A tag was still attached to the sleeve. *Galliano.* She dropped the tag as if it burned when she saw the price. How many zeroes were possible when you were only talking about a dress?

Genie picked up the next garment, and the next. All had tags. And all had cost far more than a month's wages.

She passed back into the large reception area, to find a woman laying out a teapot along with small cakes and a selection of fruit near one of the divans.

"Please, madam," the woman said. "His Majesty sends you greetings."

She indicated an envelope on the table. Genie went over and picked it up.

"Tea?"

"Um, yes. Thank you," Genie replied. It'd been hours since breakfast, and she had no idea when, or if, lunch would be served.

Ripping open the envelope, she pulled out a piece of heavy cream paper upon which Zafir had scrawled, *'Choose a dress from the closet. They were sent over for you. Dinner is at eight.'*

He'd bought the dresses for *her*? The thought was both disconcerting and warming at the same time. Disconcerting because there were so many, and they were so expensive. Warming because he'd thought to do so.

The afternoon that followed was long and lonely. Though it frustrated her to putter around the harem when she could be working, Genie still managed to soak in the hot spring, take a long nap, and find a suitable dress. The one she chose was a soft blue-gray silk with jeweled spaghetti straps. It fell right above the knee, and though it was very nice she wasn't sure she would call it sexy.

In fact she'd worked hard to find the least sexy dress she could in the lot.

But as she looked at herself in the mirror she began to wonder if she'd succeeded. The color brought out the gray of her eyes, and her coppery hair was curlier than she would have liked due to the steam in the mineral spring. The jeweled straps winked in the light, and her bare shoulders seemed too exposed while the dress clung suggestively to her breasts.

It was too late to change, however, because Yusuf had arrived to escort her to the dining room.

Except it wasn't the dining room he showed her to. Yusuf opened a door and bade her enter, then disappeared before she could ask if there was some mistake.

This room was even more ornate than the harem. There was a living area with couches, chairs, and a flatscreen television on one wall. Off to one side she could see a bedroom, with a large canopied bed. Across the room a series of arched doorways opened onto what looked like a terrace.

She was just wondering what to do when Zafir emerged from one of the darkened entryways. Her breath stopped. He'd changed out of the traditional robes and into a dark tailored suit. He wasn't wearing a tie, however, and he'd unbuttoned the first three buttons of his snowy white shirt.

She had a sudden urge to go to him, to press her mouth into that hollow at the base of his throat, to taste him the way she'd once done. He'd always tasted exotic, spicy. She'd never forgotten the way he smelled, the way his skin felt beneath her fingers. Thinking of it now was not something she wanted to do, and yet her heart wouldn't stop throwing the memories into her head.

Zafir was staring at her, his eyes moving appreciatively over her form. "You look lovely, Genie."

She tried not to blush. When was the last time she'd been dressed up? The last time a man had complimented her for the way she looked? She couldn't honestly remember. Other than a few social functions tied to funding for her projects, she didn't get out much.

"Thank you. You look pretty good yourself," she added. "I have to admit that I'm surprised you remembered my size."

"I remember a lot of things." His voice was low, suggestive. It stroked across her sensitized nerves, set up a humming in the back of her head.

But she didn't want to know what kind of things he remembered. Her pulse was already going haywire just from being here with him. To hear the things he remembered about her…?

No.

Zafir saved her by holding out a hand instead. "Come, we are dining in the courtyard."

She let him lead her outside. The courtyard was enclosed on all four sides, making it very private. There was a long table in the center, one end set with candles and flowers, the glassware and delicate china sparkling in the soft light. Flickering gas lamps provided additional light around the perimeter.

Palm trees stood nearby, their fronds sighing together where the tops towered over the enclosed walls. The breeze occasionally wafted down to the floor of the courtyard, but since darkness had settled it wasn't hot or uncomfortable.

Zafir pulled her chair out for her, then lifted her hand to his lips and pressed a kiss into her palm. Tingles radiated down her arm, over her breasts, her nipples tightening in response.

And, lower, another response gathered in her feminine core. Oh, God, she ached with want for this man. How long had it been since she'd felt this kind of heat and want?

She had to force it away, had to keep her head. It was wrong to want him when he'd hurt her so badly. She had to keep her cool, had to be all business.

"This scene is set for seduction, Zafir," she said as he took the seat opposite.

His smile was wicked with intent. "Do you think so?"

Breathe, Genie. "You know it is."

"And is it working?"

Be cool, unaffected. "I suppose that depends on what's in the food."

One eyebrow arched. "Are you suggesting I would have to drug you to succeed?"

"I'm not sure what lengths you would go to," she replied. "I hardly know you anymore."

"We could rectify that tonight, *habiba.*"

A team of waiters arrived then, saving her from a reply. One shook out her napkin and laid it across her lap, while another poured water and wine. A third man began to serve them, but Zafir said something in Arabic and the man set the dish down on the table. Then he moved the serving cart closer and bowed. The three men filed out, and once again she was alone with Zafir.

He stood and pulled the covers off the dishes. "Allow me to serve you, *habiba,*" he said.

"It's not necessary."

"No, it's not." He dished out fragrant rice, vegetables, chicken and flat bread before filling his own plate. His movements were quick, efficient, and she thought that he must not have much freedom anymore to do these sorts of things. Indeed, the waiters had looked slightly askance at their king's request they leave, but they could do nothing except obey.

"I've never been served by a king before," Genie said, taking a sip of her water.

Zafir gave her a grin as he took his seat. "Ah, but you have, many times over. I was not exactly a king then, however."

She tore off a piece of flat bread and dipped it in the sauce over the chicken. The food was aromatic, alive with spice and flavor, and she happily ate at least half of what he'd given her before she looked up and found him watching her with an amused expression.

Heat crept into her face. "This is so much better than the camp food I've been eating for the last few weeks. No matter how you try, sand seems to get into everything."

"You have been living the life of a nomad," he replied easily. "Is this what you expected to be doing when you were in school?"

"I expected to spend time in harsh places, yes." But she'd also expected more glamour and adventure. She'd soon learned, after beginning to study archaeology as an undergraduate, that the adventurous life of Indiana Jones was more than a bit exaggerated.

He cocked his head. "It is a very odd choice for such a beautiful woman. I must admit that I never envisioned you doing such things."

"No, you envisioned me in a harem."

He sighed. "I thought we were good together. I did not wish it to end simply because I had to return to Bah'shar."

Genie fixed her gaze on her plate. She'd been so naïve back then. It was humiliating to remember how happy she'd been when he'd asked her to go with him. Before she'd understood that he was not proposing marriage and never would.

"But I should have told you about Jasmin," he said. "From the beginning."

Her head snapped up. His eyes were on her. Hot, dark, intense. Did he mean it, or was this simply another attempt at seduction, at lowering her resistance?

"Yes," she said, "you should have."

Genie's eyes flashed fire as he watched her across the table. So passionate, this woman. So vibrant and alive. She had no problem challenging him, and he found he rather liked that, even while it sometimes irritated him.

"Arranged marriages, especially between royals, are such a part of my culture that I did not consider how it might affect you. Nor did I feel it necessary to explain my life to you in the beginning, when I hardly knew you."

"And now you admit you were wrong?"

"Yes." He hadn't meant to say it tonight, because he hadn't wanted her to think he was being insincere—and yet he found he needed to do so. He wanted her to understand, wanted to explain what he'd been too young and arrogant to explain that night so long ago.

"I appreciate that, but it doesn't change anything, Zafir. Even if I'd been the sort of woman who could accept such an arrangement, I wouldn't have been able to pursue my work here."

"Bah'shar is filled with ruins that need exploring by scholars. You could have done so."

She shook her head emphatically. "No, don't go there. It was impossible. I could never have accepted the kind of arrangement you were offering me."

"I know this now," he said, shoving back from the table and drawing her up from her chair.

He was growing as tired of talking about the past as she was. It did nothing but wound, and he wanted to think of other things this evening. He had enough pain in his life.

"Let us concentrate on tonight," Zafir said, pulling her close. She didn't resist as he began to sway to imaginary music. "Do you remember this?"

"Of course," she said a touch breathlessly.

They'd often danced together when the mood had hit them, and rarely had there been any music to accompany their steps.

It amazed him how right it felt to do this, how soothing it was to his senses. He'd been living in a pressure cooker for so long, yet the simplest touch from this woman relieved all the strain.

She was as light in his arms as she'd ever been. Her hair smelled exotic, like jasmine and spice, and he found himself cupping her head, threading his fingers into her short curls.

He simply had to have her, or he would die.

She leaned back to look up at him. Her fingers curled into

his lapels. "You should let me go, Zafir. Tell the Sheikh the truth and let me go back to my dig."

A dull pain pierced his heart at the thought. "Perhaps I should," he said. "But I am not going to do so."

CHAPTER FIVE

GENIE'S SENSES WERE on high alert as Zafir held her close, their bodies swaying together. The longer she was with him, the less she wanted to be anywhere else. And that was dangerous, so very dangerous.

His body was warm, hard, and her skin sizzled where his fingers rested against her back. The dress that had been so comfortable before now felt like the roughest cloth against her sensitive skin. She wanted out of it, and yet she did not. To take that step was to go down a path she'd never thought to travel again.

"I cannot believe you are here," Zafir said in her ear, his breath tickling her and sending a shiver down her spine. "I had never thought to see you again."

That his thoughts so eerily echoed hers only made her ache more.

"It would have been better that way," she said.

"I disagree." And then he kissed her, and she knew she wouldn't be able to say no if he kept kissing her this way. So sweetly, as if she was a treasure he'd discovered. So tenderly, as if she meant the world to him.

Yet she knew she didn't. This was physical and, yes, perhaps even a bit sentimental. She didn't fool herself that it was anything else. Could she handle that?

"Do you remember how it was between us? How amazing?" he asked, his breath soft against her mouth.

"Yes," she whispered.

"I want that feeling again, Genie."

His mouth fused to hers once more, and she melted away into a mass of nerve-endings that existed only to respond to his touch. Her body was on fire with remembered bliss, with the anticipation of more. It had been so long since she'd been with anyone—and now *he* was here, the man she'd never really stopped loving, and he wanted her.

And, God help her, she wanted him too. Just once. Just this once.

Because she didn't have the strength to fight herself anymore.

She slid her arms around his neck, arched into him. He groaned his appreciation, squeezed her closer. One broad hand spread over her buttocks, kneaded her, pulling the cradle of her hips against his erection. He found her most sensitive spot, his body putting pressure against hers in just the right location.

Genie gasped as sensation shot through her. Zafir slid the jeweled straps from her shoulders, his mouth finding the sensitive area where her shoulder joined her neck. It had always driven her crazy, and no doubt he remembered it.

Though how he remembered after so long was something she couldn't fathom at the moment. Not when desire and heat were tingling through her body like this.

"I need to know," she gasped, "if there's anyone else in your life right now."

He pulled back to look down at her very solemnly. "There is no one."

Genie closed her eyes as relief washed over her. If there had been a woman—a mistress, a fiancée—she could not go through with this no matter how much she ached for him. "Then touch me, Zafir."

If he didn't touch her she would die.

His voice was as warm and rich as melted honey. "I intend to, *habiba*. Most thoroughly."

When his fingers slid to her zipper, she felt a stab of apprehension. "What if someone sees us?"

His laugh against the skin of her shoulder vibrated through her body. "No one would dare. We will not be disturbed."

He spun her around and pulled her zipper all the way down. Then he slid the dress from her body. She stepped out of it, her heart hammering, her head telling her she was making a mistake, that this was too fast and too dangerous. That she was sinking into the quicksand of her need for this man, when she'd worked so hard to free herself from it the first time.

Behind her, Zafir groaned softly.

"You never wore this sort of underwear before," he said, his fingers sliding along the top edge of her thong.

Before she'd realized what he was doing, his hot mouth was on her back. His tongue dipped into the hollow at the base of her spine before he placed a kiss on her bare buttocks, and then the curve beneath where her leg began. He turned her with his hands, gazing up at her with such heat and need in his eyes that she shivered anew.

"I am a king on his knees for you," he said. "And I hardly know where to begin."

"You'll ruin your trousers." It was an inane reply, but she couldn't trust herself to say anything else.

"I do not care," he replied, reaching for her. He quickly unsnapped the clasp of her strapless bra, which fell away and exposed her bare breasts to his gaze.

Her nipples were hard, tight points, begging for his touch. Goosebumps rose on her bare flesh, but not because she was cold. Zafir licked first one tip and then the other, before suckling them into even more sensitive buds than they already were.

Genie's head fell back, her hands gripping his shoulders. She felt wanton, hot, restless, and so completely unsatisfied. Not that his mouth wasn't magical, not that she didn't love what he was doing, but she ached to feel him inside her again.

When he left her breasts and trailed hot kisses down her abdomen she sucked in her breath, knowing what he planned and dying for it all at once. Her panties fell away as he pushed them down her hips, and then he was cupping her buttocks, pulling her to him, his tongue sliding into her secret recesses finding the bud of her desire.

She cried out as he circled her clitoris, sucked it between his lips, then circled and sucked again and again. Her legs were jelly, but his strong grip on her kept her upright while he drove her to completion with his lips and tongue.

When she shattered, she didn't care who heard her as she rode wave after wave of blinding sensation.

But still it wasn't enough. And Zafir knew it too. He climbed to his feet while she sagged against the table. Shrugging out of his jacket and shirt, he dropped them to the ground. A moment later he'd lifted her onto the stone table and stepped between her legs. As she leaned back on her hands he unfastened his trousers and rolled on a condom. She didn't even bother to wonder how he'd known to be prepared.

Then he was hooking his arms behind her knees and drawing her forward until the tip of his penis slid into her entrance.

Genie drew in a sharp breath. Zafir closed his eyes, swallowed. And then he plunged forward, their bodies joining so deeply and thoroughly that they both cried out.

He grew utterly still, though she could feel him throbbing in the heart of her. "Did I hurt you?"

Genie shook her head, tears building behind her eyelids. He hurt, but not the way he meant. Physically, yes, he was big, and it had been a long time, but her body accommodated him the way it always had.

No, the pain was in her heart, her soul.

"Don't stop," she said, and then he was moving, plunging into her while she wrapped her legs around him and braced herself on the table.

She hadn't known her body could be so responsive, that she could be on fire so quickly after he'd taken her over the edge. But she gripped him hard, her hips working in time with his, her body catching the wave and riding it higher and higher.

Zafir must have sensed when she was close, because he lifted her against him, angled his thrusts so they were deeper and more intense—

And that was when she exploded, when her body dissolved into a mass of fire and sound and sensation that reached into her fingertips, her toes, her scalp. Everything sizzled, and she cried out with the intensity of it, the utter bliss.

She hadn't even realized that Zafir tumbled over the edge with her until he set her carefully back down and withdrew from her body. His skin gleamed in the candlelight, his chest rising and falling more quickly than before.

He was magnificent, exotic, and her body still craved his like a drug—though she was exhausted and, at least temporarily, sated. He turned away from her, and she felt as if she'd been basking in the sun's rays only to have a black cloud block their warmth.

What had she done?

Genie couldn't move, though she had a sudden urge to do so. It was as if her good sense had come trickling back, but too late. She wanted to snatch up the dress and cover herself.

She felt too raw, too exposed. She'd just had amazingly hot sex with a king.

On a table. In a garden.

But that wasn't what made her want to cover up. She felt as if her heart was as exposed as her body, as if he could see that it beat only for him. That it had always beat only for him.

Because this was Zafir—her prince, her lover, the man who'd once been everything to her.

And that made her angry. Angry with him for being here, for being so unrelenting, and with herself for being unable to hold fast to her vow not to have sex with him ever again. *What in the hell was wrong with her?*

"Will you let me excavate the temples now?" she threw into the air between them. Because he'd won, hadn't he? Because she was an idiot, and because she still loved him in spite of everything, and because she was suddenly so insecure that she had to lash out to protect herself.

His shoulders stiffened, and she wished with all her heart she could take it back. But words once spoken were out there, hanging in the air, and she could no more call them back than she could undo what they'd just done together.

Zafir turned, his trousers zipped again, his gaze as hard and cold as marble. He let his eyes wander over her lazily, insultingly. She pushed herself to a sitting position and wrapped her arms around herself.

"You were good, Genie. But not that good."

CHAPTER SIX

HE'D lied. Zafir lay in bed, staring up at the ornately carved wooden canopy, and listened to the soft breathing of the woman beside him. He'd told her she wasn't that good, but the truth was he'd been so hot for her that he'd been unable to make the trek to the bedroom the first time.

He'd wanted her so much that having her then and there, in the courtyard, had seemed the only way to assuage the heat boiling inside him.

Except that it hadn't. It had only made the need worse.

She might have had sex with him for the temples, but *he'd* done it because he could not do otherwise.

But Genie Gray had certainly not lost sight of what she wanted, and that made him angry.

He had no right to be angry with her. He was the one, after all, who'd suggested that the only way to win the commission was to sleep with him. He'd wanted to punish her, and he'd ended up punishing himself.

She'd pretended to be insulted, but she hadn't resisted when he'd carried her into the bedroom and made love to her again. No, she'd melted beneath him, her body as soft and welcoming as it had always been. Her body was paradise, and he lost himself in it.

They'd fallen asleep much later, exhausted, but now that he'd awakened again he couldn't get back to sleep.

What was it about her that made him so crazy? That made him feel as if he'd come home after a very long time away?

It had to be the connection to the past, to a simpler life. But this need was only temporary. Though he wanted Genie more than he could remember wanting any woman he'd ever been with, there was no future in it.

Soon he would have to let her go.

The light slanting through the curtains and across the bed was not the light of early morning. Genie blinked and sat up. Muscles she'd forgotten she had ached. Zafir had been intense last night, making love to her as if it was the first and last night he would ever do so.

The thought gave her a chill. She'd loved every moment of it, even if he had told her she wasn't that good. She'd been hurt at first, but she'd quickly recognized that he was lashing out at her. Just as she'd done when she'd asked if he would now give her the commission.

They'd gotten past that very quickly—at least physically. But now Zafir was gone and she wasn't certain what to do. Even if she did manage to find the dress and put it back on, she wasn't sure she would remember how to find the harem. And she definitely didn't want to run into anyone in the passageways.

"*As-saalamu 'alaykum*, madam."

Genie's head snapped up to find Yusuf patiently standing in the entry. He didn't seem at all flustered by her appearance in his king's bed, though she could feel the heat of a blush all the way to the roots of her hair. The problem with being a fair-skinned redhead was the ease with which she turned pink, she thought.

She returned the ritual greeting and waited.

"His Majesty bade me bring you clothing, madam. You will find a selection of items in His Majesty's bath chamber. If you would care to dress, I will bring you something to eat in half an hour."

"Thank you," Genie said, and the old man bowed and disappeared again. She waited a full five minutes before she got out of bed—stark naked—and raced into the bathroom.

When she emerged again, showered and dressed in a silk

pantsuit and ballet flats, she didn't expect to find Zafir waiting for her. Her heart did a little flip at the sight of him. He was once again dressed in traditional robes and headdress, and the sight of him literally took her breath away.

"You slept well?" he asked.

"Yes. And you?"

His grin was sudden. Wicked. "I was quite exhausted, I assure you. Thank you for a most pleasurable evening."

A most pleasurable evening.

She didn't like the way that sounded—as if she were some-one who got paid to provide a service. But then, here in this place Zafir was far more formal than she remembered him ever being when they were at university.

Perhaps that was all it was.

"And how are your negotiations with the Sheikhs going?" she asked, wanting to change the subject before she mentally undressed Zafir and climbed on top of him.

"Eager to leave?" he said, his eyes growing shadowed.

"You know I want to go back to my dig, but that's not why I asked." .

"Isn't it?" He shrugged and walked toward the small table that she only now noticed was set with plates and food. "Come, eat. And after this I will take you to the temples."

She joined him at the table, keeping her gaze from his while he once more dished out food for her. "I asked about the Sheikhs because I wanted to know," she said when he'd finished. "It seems a dangerous situation, and I hope you are able to end the hostility."

He sighed. His eyes, she noted, were troubled.

"I am working on it. In the old days I could have had them both executed. But times have fortunately progressed—even if I have often missed having that kind of absolute power while dealing with these two old fools. They grumble, but they will fall in line."

She had the distinct feeling there was something he wasn't telling her. "This isn't at all what you wanted to do, is it? Be a king, I mean?"

"It was not my choice to make."

"But if it had been?"

His dark gaze was sharp, assessing. "I would still be a Prince of Bah'shar, Genie. And I would still have duties to my nation."

And she would still be Geneva Gray, a girl who'd had to work hard for every opportunity she'd ever had. She speared a piece of mango with her fork. "I guess we can't ever change who we really are."

"No." He looked thoughtful. "But who are you inside, Genie? What can't you change?"

She swallowed. Who was she inside? She'd thought about it a lot lately, especially since coming here. "I suppose the greatest constant in my life was uncertainty."

Uncertainty over whether her father would come visit, whether her mother would make it to her school play or drop everything to be with the man she loved. Would Genie have to stand on the school steps long after the other kids had gone home and wait because her mother had forgotten again?

"I need control of my life. I get nervous when I'm not in control."

"Your parents were divorced," Zafir said, as if it explained everything.

Genie gritted her teeth. Why not tell him the truth? Why not let him see how devastating his revelation about an arranged marriage had been to her?

"That was a lie," she said, lifting her chin. "A fiction I made up in order to keep from telling anyone the awful truth."

"And what was the truth?"

She glared at him. "My mother had a decade-long affair with my father, a married man. He set her up in an apartment and came to visit us whenever he could get away from his real family."

Zafir looked stunned. "You never told me this before."

"Would it have made a difference?" she tossed at him, the old anger of her childhood and the disappointment of her relationship with Zafir mingling into an acid stew inside her.

"When my father tired of us he had no problem walking away. My mother was too depressed to go after him for child support. She took odd jobs to make ends meet, and there were times we went without heat or groceries because she barely had enough to pay the rent."

"I am sorry—"

"Yes, well, you can certainly understand why I wasn't prepared to put myself in the same position."

"I would have never abandoned you, *habiba*," he said fiercely.

"I imagine that's what my father said too."

Zafir came and sank onto a chair close by, tossing one end of his headdress over his shoulder with a practiced movement that was too sexy for words.

Sexy? Genie looked away, studied the food on her plate. How on earth could she find him sexy at a time like this?

"I would change the past if I could," he said, "but what I asked of you was not an insult in my world. I would not have forced you to stay with me once the marriage finally took place."

Genie tossed her fork aside. Now, why did that knowledge sting? "Very noble of you, Zafir."

She shoved to her feet before she lost her mind. She'd have never agreed to be a mistress, no matter what. *But isn't that what you were, Genie, considering he always intended to marry another?*

She pressed two fingers on either side of her forehead to stem the rising headache. "Look, can we just stop talking about this and get to the temples?"

"We will go soon. You need to finish eating."

"I'm not hungry. And I don't need your pity," she practically growled.

Zafir stood, his tall form suddenly towering over her. He was all formality once more, his robe draped over one arm, his eyes glittering dark and hot as he stared at her.

"As you wish, *habiba*."

CHAPTER SEVEN

THE Temples of Al-Shahar were millennia old. The foundations were ancient, though the temples in their current form were only about a thousand years old. The one temple still standing bore the soaring arches and mosaic work typical of the early Islamic period. The others were in various states of ruin, but they were all an archaeologist's dream. At the very least her team would be busy here for months. In truth, they could stay for years.

Genie walked through the structure, hands in pockets, her mind not quite as engaged as it should be for something so exciting.

Zafir was somewhere behind her, his footfalls distinct in the shadowy interior. His ever-present bodyguards had fanned out to guard the perimeter while they came inside alone. It seemed to her he'd gathered more security since yesterday. She'd asked about it, but he had shrugged the question off.

They'd hardly spoken since lunch. What was there to say?

She'd told him one of the darkest, most painful secrets of her life, and now she regretted it. Because he felt sorry for her. In Bah'shar, it seemed as if a man could have more than one family and no one thought anything of it. Not the women, not the children, and certainly not the men.

But her father had mostly ignored her existence, except for the occasional inquiry into her grades, or the awkward acceptance of a childish drawing that she'd used to believe he took home and put on the refrigerator. Now she realized he must have thrown them all out. His wife wouldn't have wanted to know anything about the woman and child he kept across town.

One day he'd finally walked out for good. She'd never known why.

Zafir passed her line of sight and she studied him from beneath the brim of her hat. She should be studying the temple, but she couldn't stop thinking about their lives together before. She replayed the kisses, the caresses, the early-morning walks, the late-night lovemaking, the look in his eyes when they'd been together—everything she could think of. How had she not realized it was only temporary?

Because it had felt like so much more. She wasn't wrong about that. She couldn't be.

But was that what her mother had thought too? Was that what had made her stay with a man who could never be hers, who'd kept her in a cage and expected her to be available whenever he wanted her?

She'd done this before, after they'd broken it off, and she was angry that she was suddenly being forced to reexamine the past after all this time. He'd accused her of needing her work more than she needed him, but it was so much more than that. Perhaps he finally realized it too.

Zafir was standing in the middle of a room, gazing down at the ruins of a mosaic on the floor. "There is much to be done here, yes?" he said, looking up and catching her staring at him.

Genie refused to look away. To do so would be to admit she'd been thinking of him and not of her work. That he'd caught her in an unguarded moment. Clearly he wasn't as tormented by thoughts of the past as she was. He'd been thinking about the temple.

"It's an extraordinary place," she said, all business. "I believe the work could take a very long time. But I also think it's a good decision to allow excavation here, even if you choose someone else to do it. This is an important site, and it should not be forgotten."

He speared her with a determined look. "I do not intend to choose someone else."

"I won't let you down if you give this to me."

"I know. It is why I made the deal in the first place."

Genie bit her lip. Whether he believed her or not, she had to say it. "I slept with you because I wanted to, not for the temples."

He waved a hand dismissively. "It matters not. The commission is yours."

She resisted the urge to stomp her foot. She'd been feeling wounded and hurt, and now he'd managed to put her on the defensive. How did he do that? "Zafir, do you believe me or not?"

He strode toward her, stopping in a swirl of robes and dust. He looked suddenly angry. "Does it matter? You have got what you want."

She swallowed as she gazed up at him, all six-foot-something of hard, arrogant male. He made her body ache just looking at him. Ridiculous the way her heart pounded. "I have never been dishonest with you, Zafir."

"Outright? No. But omission is still a form of dishonesty. You never told me what happened between your parents."

How dared he turn this around? *He* was the one at fault, not her. "What good would it have done? Besides, you were dishonest with me first."

"We were dishonest with each other."

The thought stung, and yet it wasn't the same thing at all. "Why do we keep rehashing the past? It changes nothing. You still intended to marry a woman your father chose."

"I was obligated, Genie."

She slashed a hand through the air. "I know that, and I'm done talking about it."

He caught her close, gripping her upper arms hard. "You were important to me, whether you believe it or not. And you have no idea what it is like not getting to make your own choices in life. No one has ever told *you* that you are required to give up everything you want for the greater good of your country."

Genie jerked free from his grip. She didn't fool herself that *she* was what he'd had to give up. "Maybe not, but do you think my life was any easier? *You* were born into privilege and accustomed to having the world at your fingertips. I had to work hard for every opportunity I ever got." She took a step backward, putting distance between them, her body shaking with adrenaline and fury. "What would you know about sacrifice? You wanted me to sacrifice everything to be with you, yet you weren't prepared to sacrifice a thing!"

The words echoed through the empty temple. Zafir's gaze was hard, his nostrils flaring as they stared each other down. His voice, when he finally answered, was deadly cold. "You will never know what I've sacrificed. Do not presume to tell me I have no idea what the word means."

Genie pulled in a shaky breath. Why did she get so emotional? Why did she let him press her buttons and make her so defensive? Her life had been upside down since the minute she'd walked into that tent and seen him sitting on the dais. And she was having a hell of a time getting it right again.

Zafir glanced at his watch, dismissing her as easily as he might one of his subjects. "If you are finished here, it's time we returned to the palace."

Before she could answer, he simply turned in a sweep of robes and headed toward the entrance.

He was furious. Furious with the woman sitting so quietly beside him in the car, and furious that he was allowing her to get to him when he had far more important things to think about.

Just this morning there'd been another threat to his life. He wasn't worried. His security was tight and, besides, he knew there was always a certain level of disgruntlement to be expected when a new leader took office. The threats were vague, written on plain stationery and posted in Al-Shahar. The royal police were investigating, and Zafir had every confidence they would soon find the culprit.

At least one situation in his life required definite steps to take and had a resolution in sight. For that he was thankful.

But how did one correct a situation based on strong emotion and cultural differences? If he'd known about Genie's childhood, would it have changed his actions?

Probably. Because he would have understood how painful it was to her, and would have realized how different their worlds were. He'd asked her to give up her schooling and come to Bah'shar for what amounted to nothing more than an affair.

And he'd done it for selfish reasons, which made him furious with himself. She'd filled the emptiness inside him and he'd been reluctant to give that up. And, he admitted to himself, he'd hoped that once she reached Bah'shar, once they'd been together for a while, even his marriage to a princess wouldn't prevent Genie from staying as his lover.

He'd offered her nothing and expected her to give up everything, just like she'd said.

Worse, he wanted to do it again.

When they reached the palace, he left her in the care of Yusuf and turned his attention to the Sheikhs. It was time to reach a solution. And, after that, time to let Genie Gray walk out of his life for the second time.

The rest of the afternoon passed quietly. Genie was shown to the palace library, where there was a vast selection of books, and did a bit of research on the history of Bah'shar. Her Arabic was tolerable, though her command of the Bah'sharan dialect left something to be desired, but she worked her way through a few texts as the hours passed.

She might have gotten through them more quickly if she'd been able to stop thinking about Zafir. He'd seemed unapproachable in the car on the way back to the palace, as if he'd closed himself off and meant to keep it that way.

Maybe she wouldn't see him again. Maybe he'd issue orders that she was to be driven back to her camp and left there. The thought left her feeling empty and bereft. And angry—because why did she want to torture herself by spending more time in his company?

Being sent away was the best thing that could happen to her.

She did not belong here. Oh, she would return to excavate the temples—she wasn't a fool—but she didn't belong in the royal palace in the bed of the King. Nothing good could ever come of a relationship with Zafir. She knew because she hadn't been able to stop herself from reading some of the Bah'sharan code. The King was duty-bound to take either a Bah'sharan wife or a royal one from a neighboring country. Genie, for all her success in her chosen field, had no place in his life—nor would she ever.

When she returned to the harem, she found the same servant from yesterday, who bore another letter with the King's seal. She reached for it, a thread of apprehension skimming through her.

Was this it? Was this her dismissal? She half prayed it was. The back of her neck tingled as she ripped it open and read it.

It was not a dismissal—or at least not an outright one. Zafir simply regretted that he could not have dinner with her, and indicated that she would be served in her room.

Genie ate dinner alone, then passed the evening with one of the books she'd taken from the library. She thought about going to bed several times, but she wasn't in the least bit tired, so she stayed up and read on one of the comfortable sofas. She was just about to close the book and go to bed anyway when the door to the harem opened and Zafir strode in.

A glance at her watch told her it was nearly midnight. She blinked at him in surprise.

"What are you doing here?"

He was still dressed in the garments he'd worn earlier. He jerked the headdress off and tossed it aside. "Disappointed to see me?"

Genie swallowed. "Not at all. But I thought you were angry with me."

He shrugged. "I was irritated."

"Where have you been all this time?" She winced at how

much like a jealous girlfriend she sounded. It wasn't at all wha
she'd meant to convey, but if he noticed he didn't react.

"I've been trying to make a room full of grown men stop
acting like spoiled children fighting over a toy sword."

"It's not going well, I take it?"

He popped two hands on his hips, his dark eyes full of fire
and frustration. "It could be better."

Genie closed the book and set it on the table. "I can listen i
it helps."

His gaze slid over her. "Listening is nice, but it is not wha
I want."

Her body felt as if he'd blazed a trail of flame over it.

"What do you want?"

His grin was sexy, sinful. "A swim in the mineral bath."

"Oh," she said, sudden disappointment swirling inside
her. She shouldn't want to make love with him again, but she
couldn't stop the desire coursing in her veins like thick syrup
Just as well he didn't seem affected by it.

"You may join me, if you wish." He left her sitting there, he
mouth dropping open, as he headed for the spa. Genie debate
with herself for a full minute before getting up and following
him.

Zafir stood poolside, stripping out of his garments. He
mouth went dry as layer after layer was peeled away until he
stood there bronzed, hard-muscled, and magnificently naked
He wasn't fully aroused, but he was on his way.

She should turn and walk away, should prove to herself and
to him that she was capable of refusing to be drawn into anothe
doomed relationship with him. Last night had been amazing
a reminder of all she'd missed for so long. Did she really nee
another when there was no future in it?

"Coming in?" he asked, before he dove cleanly into the
water. He came up like a dolphin, rivulets of water rushing
down his chest and arms before he flipped over and started t
backstroke across the pool.

Was she? Could she really turn away and go back to her book
when all this glorious male body waited for her? She stood there

indecision, until Zafir cupped his hands and splattered her
ith water from halfway across the pool.

Genie began to unbutton her shirt. "You're going to pay for
at," she said.

Zafir swam toward her, his eyes glittering with heat and
esire. "I look forward to it."

She stripped, and would have glided into the pool quietly
d he not shot up and grabbed her. He threw her over his head
d she went under.

When she came up, sputtering, he was laughing. "A little
ow, aren't you?"

Genie dove under and went for his feet. She jerked them out
om under him and he splashed down while she powered away
 the other side of the pool. But before she made it strong arms
circled her and hauled her back against his body.

The length of his erection pressed against her buttocks. Her
sides liquefied.

"You give as good as you get, don't you, *habiba*?" he growled
 her ear. But it was a sensual growl, not an angry one.

"I try," she replied, her pulse zipping into light speed. My
od, it took nothing at all for this desire to spiral out of control.
e should have known it would.

"Mmm, and I can think of so many ways to test your ability
 get even with me." He turned her in his arms, his slick skin
t against hers. Part of it was the natural heat of the spring,
d part was the desire between them.

Genie wrapped her arms and legs around him, feeling sud-
nly reckless and full of joy.

"You are welcome to try, King Zafir. I relish the op-
rtunity."

"Do you indeed?"

In answer, she kissed him, urgently tangling her tongue with
s. Zafir responded as she'd hoped, groaning and squeezing
r to him. His hands wandered, his fingers sliding around her
ttom, down to the vee of her legs. He stroked her center lightly
d she rocked against him, trying to make him go faster.

He only laughed low in his throat, however. Genie reached

for him, wrapped her hand around his hard length and squeeze
His laugh turned to a moan.

She broke the kiss, trailed her tongue down his throat, h
chest—and then she sank beneath the water and took him
her mouth. His thigh muscles tightened and she could feel t
sharp intake of his breath where one of her hands rested agai
his abdomen.

The other stroked him while she swirled her tongue arou
his length. Soon, however, he grabbed her and hauled her u

"I could have held my breath for another minute," s
grumbled.

"But I'm not sure I could have held mine," he said. "I decl
you the winner of this round, because I am now unwilling
wait."

He took her by the waist and lifted her from the pool. Th
he leapt out beside her and hauled her over to one of the cus
ioned divans that lined the sides of the chamber. "This is mu
more comfortable," he murmured, following her down.

There were no preliminaries. There was no need. Gen
wrapped her legs around him as he sank into her. Her he
tilted back, her eyes closing tight as the bliss of his possessi
threatened to overwhelm her. "Zafir," she gasped.

His lips were on her throat, her jaw, her breasts.

"I cannot get enough of you, Genie," he said, almost br
kenly. "The more I have, the more I want."

And then he was thrusting into her, hard and fast, hurtli
her toward the abyss. She welcomed it, wanted it, craved it-

Suddenly she was there, crying out his name and wonderi
how it was possible to feel this way with only one person
the whole world. To feel as if you needed this to live, as if y
would die if you didn't have it.

It was beautiful and heartbreaking all at once. She was
love with a man she could never have. Even if she gave
everything and moved to Bah'shar to be with him she wo
only have stolen moments of bliss like this one.

And that wasn't nearly enough.

CHAPTER EIGHT

ZAFIR'S brain had dissolved along with his sense. He rolled
from her body, belatedly remembering as he came back to earth
that he'd forgotten to use a condom. Icy cold fear dripped down
his spine in spite of the heat in the room. How could he be so
stupid?

How could he risk such a thing?

Because this was Genie, and she excited him, made him
forget everything but the urge to join himself with her. She
always had, though she'd been on the pill when they were at
university. He prayed that was still the case.

"Are you on birth control?" he asked, his tone sharper than
he'd intended.

She blinked at him, her expression confused. And then it
cleared. Horror was not the emotion he'd hoped to see. She
sat up and wrapped her arms around her knees, her skin still
flushed from sex and dripping with water from the pool.

"I am, but I haven't had a pill in two days now. All my things
were in the camp…"

Zafir swore.

"It's the wrong time of the month, though. I'm sure of it."

"If there is a baby, I want to know," he ordered. "I will provide for him, never fear, so there is no need to terminate the
pregnancy."

Her lovely face clouded. When it cleared, anger was the
dominant emotion. "Of course I would tell you, Zafir. What
kind of person do you think I am?"

He thought of Layla, of her deception, and his jaw tightene
"You are a professional woman. Perhaps you would decide th
a baby was too much of a burden for you."

"It wouldn't be easy, I grant you. But if there were a chil
it would be ours. And I would want it."

She looked so fierce that he believed her. The relief windi
through him was stronger than he would have believed possibl
And he felt a sudden need to explain, to share with her wh
he'd never told anyone else.

"My second wife aborted our child. She did not tell me sh
was pregnant."

Genie's eyes widened. "I'm so sorry, Zafir. You must ha
been very upset."

"I was. Layla felt she was too young to start a family, thoug
she failed to share this belief with me."

She had also been worried about her figure, her shoppi
trips abroad, and her social events, where she was determin
to be the most elegant hostess anyone in Bah'shar had ev
seen. When she'd gone to Europe for the abortion he'd thoug
she was going on another shopping trip. He'd only found o
because she'd been stupid enough to use a credit card and he
opened the bill before she could intercept it. The moment wh
he'd realized what the charge was for had been like a suck
punch to the gut.

Genie put her arms around him and squeezed. He fell ba
on the cushions with her, his heart hammering with fear, a
turned his head toward her, breathed in the sweet, clean sce
of her hair.

She smelled like home, felt like home. He could think
nothing better than watching her grow big with his chil
Nothing better than having her in his bed every night.

"I'm sure there's nothing to worry about," she said softl
"but if I'm wrong, this is your child too. We'll figure out wh
comes next when we have to."

"Yes, we'll figure it out," he replied on a sigh of wearines
It had been a long, long day.

He closed his eyes. What he needed right now was sleep. And he needed to be here with this woman.

It felt right.

He was drifting off when she whispered in his ear, "Sleep, Zafir."

She said something else, but he wasn't quite certain what it was.

Right before he fell asleep, he realized what it had sounded like: *I love you.*

Sometime in the night they got chilled and moved into the bedroom, burrowing beneath the thick covers on the bed. Genie lay in the dark, listening to Zafir's deep breathing. She was in so much trouble here. In two days' time her life had been turned inside out by the past she'd tried to forget.

She still loved him, and she couldn't deny it. And, though she really didn't believe she could fall pregnant, the slight chance had her mind working overtime. What would happen if she had his baby?

He'd said he would provide for their child. But he wasn't going to offer to marry her. He was the King of Bah'shar and he could never do so.

But would he be a part of their child's life? Or would he, like her father, be absent and distant?

Genie didn't believe Zafir would ignore their child on purpose. He would not be like her father. But his royal duties and his future wife—because, yes, a king needed legitimate heirs—would most likely keep him away.

Genie shifted in the bed, trying to shove her tumultuous thoughts away. There was nothing to worry about *yet*. She would cross that bridge when she reached it.

"Can't sleep?"

"Not well," she admitted. "You?"

"I was sleeping fine, but you kept moving."

"Sorry."

She heard him yawn. "You are worried about being pregnant?"

"I was thinking about it, yes. But I don't really believe it will happen."

"You will not have to worry, Genie."

"No, but I think I'll have to worry every day of my life if there's a child. That's just what mothers do." She turned toward him on the bed, propped herself on an elbow. "I'm sorry about what happened with your second wife, Zafir."

"It was a long time ago."

She bit her lip, decided to proceed. "What happened in your first marriage?"

Zafir did not pretend to misunderstand what she was asking him. He let out a deep sigh. "Jasmin had difficulty conceiving. When she did conceive, she couldn't carry past the first trimester."

"I'm so sorry."

"There were three miscarriages. She was depressed, though I did not realize it, and she swallowed pills. It is my fault she died. I should have forced her into treatment."

Sadness ripped through her. "How could you know she would do such a thing?"

"I should have known. She was impulsive, and she made threats. I didn't take her seriously until I came home late and found her unconscious." He sighed into the darkness. "I wasn't supposed to be late that day. I think she wanted to be found, that it was a cry for help. But I failed her."

My God. Genie's eyes filled with tears. How could he take such a burden on himself? But she already knew the answer: he was a good man who took his duty seriously, be it the duty of a king or a husband. Or even a lover.

"If there's one thing I learned growing up," she said very softly, "it's that we aren't responsible for the actions of others. My mother and I both suffered because she wouldn't—or couldn't—get herself out of the situation with my father, but that wasn't my fault. It took me a long time to understand that."

"I knew Jasmin was unstable. I should have realized she would eventually go through with her threats."

Genie grasped his hand in hers. It was big, warm, and he

squeezed his fingers closed around her hand. The grip was firm, reassuring, but not too hard. A wave of love and longing rocked through her.

"No one is to blame but her, Zafir. I'm sorry if that sounds harsh, but she is responsible for making that choice, not you."

"If I'd been home when expected—"

"You could have stopped her that time, but what about the next? Maybe she could have been helped with treatment, but there are no guarantees. You're wrong to blame yourself."

He pulled her hand to his lips. "You have grown wise, Dr. Gray. Thank you for your words, though I am certain I will always feel guilty about what happened."

"That's your right, Zafir." It made her sad that he would take so much on himself, and sad for his poor wife. It also made her feel badly for resenting Jasmin for so long. She'd been caught up in the marital politics of her people as much as Zafir had been. And producing an heir had no doubt been paramount to that marriage. When she hadn't been able to do so, she must have felt so desperate.

Genie burrowed in closer, wrapped her arms around him. Her heart was a lost cause and it did no good to try and keep her distance. She would take whatever time she had with him while it lasted.

He stroked the skin of her bare back, his fingers dipping farther and farther down her spine each time. Liquid heat filled her veins, but she would not act on it. This was about comfort, not sex.

Until he shifted and she realized he was fully aroused. "Wait a minute," he said, leaving the bed and then returning before she'd had a chance to miss his heat. She heard the rip of foil, and then he was on top of her, pressing inside her slick body while she moaned her pleasure to the heavens above.

They'd had a few days of bliss, but Zafir knew it would have to end. The problem was that he didn't want to let her go. That having her here seemed like the most important thing in the world. With Genie in his life, his bed, his heart, he faced each

day with the determination and strength he needed to make
Bah'shar better than ever.

She made this life that had been thrust upon him make sense.
He'd married twice, out of duty, but he'd never felt as if he'd
had a connection with either of his wives. Why did he feel this
connection with a woman he could never have?

He could never ask her to give up her life for him—not now.
She was a professional, successful woman. And he was still
required to marry and produce heirs for the throne.

But why couldn't he marry *her*? She could still do her work,
and she would come home to him each night. She'd said the
temples could take years…

"Your Majesty?"

Zafir shook himself. The men gathered around the confer-
ence table were staring at him.

"Please repeat that," he said smoothly. The meeting continued, and Zafir worked to concentrate on what was being said.
After nearly fifteen minutes of circular logic, his mind drifted
once more.

He couldn't stop picturing Genie in a traditional Bah'sharan
bridal gown.

Though Bah'sharan law did not allow for a foreign wife who
was not a princess, the law was old and could be changed. It
had been meant to protect the throne from overthrow, but that
was not so much an issue in today's world.

It wouldn't be easy, and there would no doubt be much grum-
bling and arguing amongst his ministers, but changing the code
was possible. The idea galvanized him.

Raised voices brought him sharply back to the present.
Sheikh Abu Bakr had gone to stand by a window with his
back to the group. Sheikh Hassan sat with his arms crossed
and a militant expression on his face. Zafir's ministers looked
exasperated.

Zafir had had enough for now.

"Let us take a break," he interjected. "I will return in an
hour's time, and I expect you all to be here, ready to talk."

He stood. Everyone in the room shot to their feet and bowed.

Zafir turned and strode out the door. There was just enough time to see Genie, maybe have a little lunch with her. He wouldn't tell her about his idea just yet. It was too new, and he was still too uncertain it was the correct path. His heart believed it was, but his head needed time to adjust.

There was a shortcut to the harem and he took it, passing down long dark corridors that were rarely used anymore. He was excited about the idea of changing the code, about talking Genie into marrying him and staying in Bah'shar, but he was torn as well. Though it felt like the best solution for him personally, was it best for his people? For his nation?

As he passed a dark alcove, a sharp pain sliced across his arm. Zafir spun as something flashed silver in the dim light. All his senses were on high alert as the assassin's knife descended again.

"Die, traitor," a voice breathed as the knife plunged home.

CHAPTER NINE

GENIE was in the library, researching the Temples of Al-Shahar, when two men in dark clothes burst in. She recognized them as being on Zafir's security team from the Uzis slung across their chests and the microphones in their ears. She didn't even realize she'd gotten to her feet until they crashed to a halt in front of her.

"You will come with us," one of the men said.

"Where are we going?" She'd faced menacing characters before in her line of work, but these two made her heart pound a little harder than usual. Perhaps because they were part of the team that ensured Zafir's safety. If they were here, was something wrong? Was there danger?

A tremor of apprehension snaked along her spine.

"The hospital."

"But what has happened?" she said as they hustled her toward the exit.

One of the men looked down at her with a grave expression. "The King has been stabbed."

Zafir winced as the doctor probed at the wound.

"You are lucky, Your Majesty," he said. "It's only a flesh wound."

Yes, but one that hurt like hell. And one that he would not have gotten had he not been distracted by thoughts of the woman he'd been in a hurry to see again.

"A few stitches and it will heal nicely," the doctor continued as he finished his examination.

The man went to get his supplies and Zafir turned to the guard who stood silently by.

"Is she here yet?"

"They are bringing her now, Majesty."

A moment later the door burst open and Genie rushed in. He was no longer surprised at the kick in the gut he felt when he saw her, but he pushed it down deep and put a lid on it. She was pale and her cheeks were tear-streaked. He took in her puffy eyes, her red nose, and felt a pang of guilt.

He had to let her go. For her safety. Until the moment he'd been attacked he hadn't stopped to think how his people might react to a Western woman as their queen. There were those who would never accept it. Though it made him want to howl in frustration to be forced to give up happiness just when he'd thought he might have found it, he had to do so.

For her. What he wanted didn't matter when contrasted with the risk to her life.

Because who was to say that she would not be the target of an assassination attempt at some point? She would be resented by those who didn't want change, and she might draw the wrath of extremist groups.

He could not allow that. Not ever.

"Zafir," she gasped, rushing over to him. She stopped short when she saw the bloody wound on his arm. Then her gaze lifted to his. Her voice wavered. "They said you'd been hurt."

Not as hurt as the assassin he'd disarmed. "I am fine, Genie. It's not serious."

He wanted to hold her, reassure her. But he would not. Keeping his arms at his sides was one of the toughest things he'd ever had to do.

"Do you know who did it?" Her eyes were huge pools of rainwater gray and tears trembled on the brink of her lashes.

"Oh, yes. The conspirators will be dealt with, I assure you." Once the would-be assassin had realized he'd failed, he'd spilled his guts to the police.

Zafir said a quiet word to the bodyguard. The man went to stand outside the door.

Once he was gone, Genie reached for Zafir's hand. "I couldn't bear the thought of losing you—"

"Genie," he cut in before she could say more. He must have spoken sharply because she fell quiet instantly. He squeezed her hand before letting it go. How could he do this? How could he send away the only bit of happiness he'd ever known? He drew in a painful breath. "I am sending you back to your camp."

She bit her lip, confusion playing across her expressive face. Her guard was down and every emotion she felt was there to read in detail. It pained him to look at her, but he would not look away.

"Now? Today?"

He nodded. "You have fulfilled your end of the bargain, and I will fulfill mine. You are free to go. Yusuf will give you all you need for contacting the proper authorities for the excavation. They will be told to cooperate fully."

She looked stunned. "I... I... Why, Zafir? Why now?"

His heart was a lead ball in his chest. "It is time."

"Does this mean you've concluded your negotiations with the Sheikhs?"

"Yes," he said. "It is done." Done because one of their number had tried to kill him in order to frame the other group for murder. The leaders were so horrified they would now do anything to demonstrate their loyalty. And he meant to take advantage of it.

"That's good. Congratulations."

"There is much work yet to be done, and you have served your purpose." She winced when he said that, and he mentally kicked himself for it. "I can ask no more of you."

"Is this your revenge?" she asked. "Making me care for you again and then sending me away?"

The words pierced him. For a brief moment he thought it might be easier to let her believe that, but he couldn't do it.

"No, Genie, this is not revenge. We are two different people now, from two different worlds, and it's time we got back to them."

She took a deep breath. "Yes, I suppose you're right. I—" She swallowed "It was great to see you again."

"I enjoyed our time together." A hard lump had formed in his throat and made it difficult to speak. He ignored it. Letting her go was right. For her, for him. She didn't belong here, and he needed to get back to the business of governing his kingdom.

He thought of her swollen with his child. It nearly overwhelmed his will to release her. "I trust you, Genie. You will tell me if there is a child?"

"Of course," she said, all business. "I would never keep that information a secret from you."

"Yusuf will give you my private number. Call me when you know."

She nodded. "Absolutely. If that's all, then? The sooner I get back to camp, the sooner I can get to work again."

She stood stiffly, like a soldier. Even her hands had disappeared behind her back. He imagined her clasping them together with military precision. She was already leaving him in her mind. How easily she returned to the life she'd led before.

Perhaps his had been the only heart affected after all.

"Goodbye, Genie."

"Goodbye, Zafir." And then she was gone.

First came numbness. Then shock. Then anger. Then resignation.

When Zafir decided to get rid of her, he certainly did it in style. A helicopter waited on the pad at the palace. Genie took one last look behind her before she climbed in, her heart aching. Did she really think he would suddenly appear and ask her to stay?

She shook her head, wondering how a few days with him had so thoroughly undermined the foundations of her life. She was a respected archaeologist and researcher, and the sooner she got back to that life, the better.

As the craft lifted off, she kept her eyes on the glittering domes of the palace. It was like something out of a fairytale—from a thousand and one Arabian nights. Unlike Scheherazade, however, she'd failed to please her king for more than a few nights.

She still couldn't believe that he'd dismissed her from his life so easily. That everything that had happened between them meant nothing. Or maybe she'd let it mean more than it should.

But he'd touched her so tenderly, made love to her so fiercely. Claimed to want her desperately.

Had it all been a lie?

She watched the cloudless sky slide by and wished she'd never come to the desert.

Another lesson learned, Genie.

She supposed she should be thankful he'd ended it now, before she'd made a fool of herself and babbled her love. Before she'd mentally set up house with him and let her career fall by the wayside.

Her mother had been right, in her own way. A man would take your love and then set you adrift to pick up the pieces of your shattered life when he was finished with you.

She should be grateful the only pieces she had to pick up were the pieces of her heart.

When she reached the camp, she threw herself into work. Her colleagues were glad to see her, and they'd done much to repair the damage the last few days had wrought. The dig was well under control when Genie finally decided she'd had enough.

Al-Shahar was two hours away by car, and she couldn't stop looking for Zafir. She kept thinking he would arrive in a convoy of black vehicles, that he would climb out of a stretch Hummer, looking magnificent and exotic in his desert robes, and that he would tell her he'd made a mistake. That he wanted her to come back and be with him—that he loved her.

Any lingering hope she'd harbored that she might see him once more if she were with child was dashed early one morning when she got her period as usual. That was the final matter that settled it for her. She made the call to his private line, left a message—had she really expected Zafir to pick up?—and told her team she was flying home to begin preparations for their next dig.

It would be some weeks before they were ready to fly to Al-Shahar and begin work on the temples. But on the long flight across the Atlantic Genie came to another decision.

She would not be returning to Bah'shar.

CHAPTER TEN

THE weeks that dragged by seemed to last forever, but Zafir knew she would return soon. Genie would not abandon the temples. She might have pushed him from her life easily enough once he'd sent her away, but the temples would lure her back.

And he wanted to see her. Needed to see her. She was still a fire in his blood, no matter that he'd tried to convince himself otherwise. He'd sent her away for her safety, and yet he couldn't wait until she returned.

He remembered her voice on the message she'd left him. She'd sounded so tough, so businesslike as she'd informed him there was no baby. The words had jarred him, and yet it was the outcome that was the best for them both.

He'd thrown himself into work over the past weeks. The tension in the border region remained higher than he'd like, but it was difficult to eradicate years of mistrust in only a few months. There had been no violence, no raids, and he was pleased with the two Sheikhs' commitment to peace.

He'd also been looking at the code of law, and he'd made changes there as well. He'd brought new business to the capital by offering trade incentives, and he'd met with local business leaders and politicians to determine what their needs were for growth and stability.

He'd traveled extensively over the last month, expanding Bah'shar's ties to the world, but no amount of work had been enough to erase Genie Gray from his mind.

Soon she would be in Bah'shar again. And he would go to see her.

He knew precisely when the team of archaeologists arrived for their excavation. He'd kept out of the arrangements with the Ministry of Culture, but that date was something he'd had Yusuf find out for him. He waited two days past their arrival before he ordered a car and went to the temples.

The ruins were a hive of activity that ceased immediately upon his arrival. A plump, graying man in khaki trousers and a dirt-streaked shirt hurried over.

"Your Majesty," he said, bowing low. "We are honored by your presence."

"You are happy with the arrangements?" Zafir asked politely.

"Indeed, we couldn't be more pleased. Everyone has been marvelous."

Zafir talked with the man who introduced himself as Dr. Dan Walker for a few moments more, scanning the site for any sign of Genie. None of the women he saw could be the feisty redhead he sought.

"Excuse me," Zafir said, cutting into Dr. Walker's excited chatter about mosaics and pottery shards, "but where is Dr. Gray?"

The man blinked. "Oh, I'm sorry. Dr. Gray did not accompany us."

Zafir frowned. "She is coming later, then?"

Dan Walker's pudgy cheeks glistened with perspiration. "Dr. Gray has opted to teach at university this semester, sir. She will not be a part of this excavation."

The October air was crisp in Massachusetts, but the trees were absolutely gorgeous, their leaves turning various shades of gold and red that took her breath away. Caldwell University was a prestigious private institution with a long history and a top archaeology program, and Genie had come here as a guest lecturer for the semester. After that she wasn't certain what she planned to do. There was a dig in China coming up, and she was thinking about signing on for it.

She thought of her teammates in Bah'shar, of the temple and all they would learn. She envied them, and yet she knew she'd made the right decision. If she'd returned to Bah'shar she wouldn't have been able to give her work the full concentration it deserved.

No, she'd have kept looking toward the palace and daydreaming about a desert king in white robes, riding an Arabian stallion. As if she didn't do enough of that already. A week in Bah'shar with Zafir had ruined her for another ten years at least. She'd never stopped loving him, and she could never be with him. What would it take to forget him?

Death, probably.

The bell rang and her students slapped their books closed and dashed out. As her next class filtered into her room, she made a few notes about the text and what she'd discovered while teaching it.

A group of girls gathered by one of the windows. No doubt the latest, greatest university quarterback was strolling by outside. Tim Robbins? Tom Ribbens? Rob Timmens? She couldn't remember, and didn't really care—though a smile lifted one corner of her mouth as she remembered her own days at university.

She'd had a crush on a football player for all of three weeks before Zafir bin Rashid al-Khalifa, the new man on campus, strode into a frat party and rocked her world. Nothing had been the same since.

When it was time to begin class, the girls were still at the window, their chatter low and excited.

"Take your seats, ladies," Genie said. "We have a lot to cover today."

"There's the most amazing sight out here, Dr. Gray."

"Yes, I'm sure that's true, but please, let's get to work." Genie used her best stern teacher voice, which seemed to do the trick.

The girls sat down and Genie stood up to begin her lecture

Movement outside caught her eye, and she glided toward the window as casually as possible while beginning to explain the complexities of identifying human bones and the importance of cataloguing them properly.

A long car sat against the curb, and four men in dark suits with radio transmitters flanked it. There was a police car in front and back, and both had their flashing lights on. She could see a cop talking on the radio in the first car.

Perhaps the Governor was visiting the school. Or Senator Hall. His daughter attended Caldwell.

Genie made the trip back to the whiteboard and picked up the marker. She was just beginning to write a few notes on the board when the door swung open. A man who bore the distinct mark of a bodyguard walked into the room, and then another followed. They flanked the door and Genie turned to her students, wondering if Senator Hall's daughter was in her class and she'd somehow forgotten it.

She turned back just as a tall, dark man in an expensive suit walked in. He was handsome and regal and he fixed her with a hawk-like stare. Her heart skidded to a stop in her chest before beginning to beat double time. There was a collective intake of breath from her classroom. The girls, no doubt.

"What are you doing here?" Genie blurted.

Zafir's sensual mouth turned down in a frown. "I have come a long way to speak with you, Dr. Gray. I had hoped your welcome would be more...appropriate."

Appropriate? What on earth was he talking about? If a Martian had walked off his spaceship and into her classroom she couldn't have been more surprised than she was right now.

She looked at her students, wondering if perhaps she was hallucinating. Surely their confused expressions would confirm he was crazy.

But the girls were staring at Zafir in open-mouthed admiration; the young men were looking at him with curiosity.

"Class," she said, trying to salvage the session and her dignity at the same time, "this is His Majesty King Zafir bin Rashid

al-Khalifa of the Kingdom of Bah'shar. We are honored to hav
you, Your Majesty."

Zafir inclined his head, as if he'd fully expected to be we
comed like a visiting potentate. "May I speak with you privatel
Dr. Gray?" he said, never missing a beat.

"As you can see, class has just begun. You'll have to com
back later."

"Ah—please excuse the interruption. But if you don't mind
he said, his polite smile turning devilish, "I would like t
listen."

His arrogance made her waspish. What was he doing here
How could she ever put him behind her if he kept popping u
when she least expected it? "I'm afraid we don't have a thron
available for you to sit on."

He shrugged. "There is a chair behind your desk. I will s
there."

Genie fumed. She didn't know why he was here and it irrita
ed her. He'd dismissed her from his life so easily, so coldly, an
now he was here, in her classroom, larger than life. Why?

No matter how she tried to ignore it, little bubbles of joy wer
popping in her veins like champagne fizz. She didn't trust th
feeling, however.

She didn't trust him.

"By all means. Make yourself at home."

Zafir crossed to the desk and took a seat, and Genie turne
back to the board. She soldiered on with the lecture for the ne
forty-five minutes, though she deliberately did not look at Zaf
again. She could feel his eyes burning into her, and she ke
hoping he would get bored and leave.

But he stayed until the class was over. Several of the girl
lingered over their desks, laboriously putting their books an
laptops away. Once they were gone, she turned to him.

"What is this all about?" she demanded, hands on hip
frustration and confusion zipping around inside her.

Zafir stood, his easy demeanor gone. He looked mildl
angry. "The Temples of Al-Shahar. I wanted you to lead th
team, but you did not come."

She looked away. "I thought better of it."

"We made a deal, Genie."

"No, *you* made a deal. As I recall, I didn't have much choice."

"I wanted you," he repeated.

"Dr. Walker is fully qualified. Hell, he's more qualified than I am, if that's what you're worried about."

Zafir took a step toward her. "I wanted you."

"We don't always get what we want, Zafir."

He closed the distance between them. "I wanted you."

He stood so close, the heat of his body reaching out to envelop her. He smelled exotic, spicy, and she remembered running her tongue along his skin. She gave herself a mental shake. "I get it, Zafir. You wanted me to lead the dig, and now you're angry because you didn't get your way."

"No," he cut in, "I wanted you. You, Genie Gray."

"Why do you keep saying that?" she cried. She whirled away from him, intending to put distance between them.

But he caught her, pulled her against his hard body. "Genie," he said in her ear, "I want you."

And then she understood. He loosened his grip and she turned in his arms, pulling away when he didn't try to keep her.

"You came all this way for sex?"

His laugh was unexpected. "I came for you. Come to Bah'shar with me, Genie."

Her heart was thundering in her ears. "Why would I want to do that?" she whispered.

"Because you love me."

She closed her eyes. Swallowed. "I do love you," she said. "But it's not enough, Zafir."

"And what if I said I loved you too?"

"I can't come with you, Zafir," she said, shaking her head. "I can never settle for being second best in your life. I can't believe you would ask me this again—"

"I want you to be my queen," he cut in.

He looked lost, uncertain, and her heart contracted with pain and love.

"You can't mean that," she said. "It's impossible."

"Why? Because of your career?"

Was he that obtuse? Did he have to make her say it? "No, because of you. It's Bah'sharan law—"

"Not any longer," he said fiercely.

Genie blinked, dumbfounded. "You changed the law?"

"It was an old law, and it made no sense. The people agreed."

"You had a vote?"

"Yes."

Her heart was beginning to believe, but her head couldn't quite accept it. "But how do you know you really love me? That it's not just attraction and—?"

Zafir groaned. "My God, woman, do you think that I couldn't find a willing female to have sex with in Bah'shar if that was my only problem? That I've flown halfway around the world to get down on my knees and beg, if that is what it takes, for you to come to Bah'shar with me simply because I have an uncontrollable erection?"

In spite of the seriousness of the situation she wanted to laugh suddenly. Somehow she managed not to. "When you put it like that…"

He looked offended. "Exactly."

"Then why did you send me away after you were stabbed?" It still hurt that he had done so, and she wanted to understand. "I was so scared for you, and you dismissed me as if it meant nothing."

"I know, and I'm sorry. But there had been threats against my life, and when I was attacked I realized that I had put you in danger too. I couldn't live with that. Your safety is the most important thing in the world to me." He blew out a breath. "But now you aren't there, and I still think of you constantly. I need you, Genie. Without you, I'm only half the king I should be."

"I'm not afraid of a little danger," she said a touch unsteadily. The conversation seemed so unreal that she was having a hard time processing all the implications. "Being an archaeologist can be dangerous at times."

"I know, but this danger was different. And though there may always be some degree of danger when one lives such a public life, I am confident the people of Bah'shar will love you as I do."

"I don't want to give up archaeology entirely," she said. "I love what I do."

"I understand this," he replied. "Just as I want to build things, you want to dig in the dirt. But there is much to excavate in Bah'shar. And if you need to go elsewhere on your digs, we will work it out."

She couldn't believe she was hearing this. The man she loved was standing here, offering her everything she'd ever wanted, and she was scared. Scared she was missing something, or that there was a catch somewhere. Could she really be Queen of Bah'shar?

"I'm not sure I'm cut out for this, Zafir."

He didn't need to ask what she meant. "I wasn't supposed to be a king," he said, "but I'm learning. You will learn too."

Genie's heart was swelling, daring to hope, daring to believe.

How could she not take the leap? She had to. *Had to.* She loved this man with all her heart and she didn't want to let him go ever again. She'd be queen of anything if that was what it took.

"You're sure you really love me?"

He put his hands on her shoulders, bent to look her in the eye. "Dr. Geneva Gray, I love you. Only you. Forever you. Come to the desert with me. Be my wife, bear my children, grow old with me."

A tremor passed through her. It was real. He was real.

"Kiss me, Zafir," she said.

"Gladly."

The kiss was everything she'd hoped. It was the kiss of a man who loved her. Happiness flooded her soul with sunshine, breaking through all the pain and emptiness of the last few weeks.

"I love you, Zafir. This time you can't get rid of me."

"Exactly as I'd hoped," he said, before kissing her again.

EPILOGUE

One year later...

KING ZAFIR BIN RASHID AL-KHALIFA was in a hurry. He strode through the palace corridors at a pace that had the staff scurrying out of his way. Finally he burst into the royal apartments and kept going until he found his wife in the bathroom, removing her soiled clothing.

Genie looked up when he came in, her face creasing in a smile that did odd things to his heart. Dirt and mud streaked her fair skin. Her hair, spiked with drying sweat, stood at odd angles from her head.

Zafir thought she'd never looked more beautiful. "You are home early, *habiba*," he said.

She continued to remove clothing, dropping it in a pile at her feet. The more of her luscious body that was revealed, the more his own body responded. Oh, yes, he was definitely going to have her.

In the shower. On the bed. Perhaps even the floor if he couldn't make it to the bed first.

"I was feeling a bit tired," she said.

Zafir frowned. "But you went to bed early last night. I remember this quite well. Did you awaken?"

"No, I slept straight through." The last of her clothing fell in a *poof* of dust. She reached for the taps and turned on the shower. Zafir worked hard to make his brain function. Her gorgeous pink nipples were ripe for his touch. He needed to touch them. Needed to taste them.

Marrying Genie was the best decision he'd ever made. Not just because he needed her with a fierceness that hadn't abated in the last twelve months, but also because she made him whole. She filled his life and took away every ounce of loneliness he'd ever felt.

She was the other half to his soul.

"I have sent for the doctor," she continued, and Zafir's heart dropped to his toes. She was his greatest treasure, his reason for being. She could not be ill.

"Doctor?"

"Don't look so worried," she said, coming over and giving him a quick squeeze while trying not to soil his clothing at the same time. "It's nothing serious."

"You can't know that. You aren't a doctor—" He stopped, amended the statement when she arched an eyebrow. "Not *that* kind of doctor."

She walked into the steamy shower and stood under the spray. "I simply need him to confirm something for me."

Why would she need a doctor to confirm…?

And then it hit him. His knees felt suddenly weak, his heart thudding into his throat. He realized that Genie had opened her eyes and was watching him.

"Are you…? Do you mean…?" He couldn't find the words.

Genie smiled and opened her arms. "Why don't you join me?"

He ripped off his clothes and stepped under the spray, taking her into his arms. "No more digging in the dirt in the middle of the hot day, Genie," he ordered. "And no more crawling into dank tombs beneath the temples."

"Yes, Your Majesty," she said. "Besides, I doubt I'll be able to get inside those narrow spaces in the next few months anyway."

"I love you," Zafir said. "More than you can ever imagine."

Her eyes sparkled. "Oh, I can imagine a lot."

"So can I, thanks to you."

And then he proceeded to show her the depths of his very creative imagination.

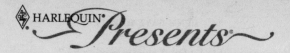

Coming Next Month

Coming Next Month